Dreams of the Woman Who Loved Sex

tee corinne

Dreams
of the
Woman
Who
Loved
Sex

a collection

BANNED BOOKS
Austin, Texas

ISBN 0-934411-05-0

Passages from these stories are reprinted from PLEASURES Women
Write Erotica, Lonnie Barbach, ed., copyright 1984; EROTIC
INTERLUDES, Tales Told by Women, Lonnie Barbach, ed., copyright
1986; On Our Backs and Yoni. Poems by Yosano Akiko and Yamakawa Tomiko are published in WOMEN POETS OF JAPAN, copyright
1977 by Kenneth Rexroth and Ikuko Atsumi, A New Directions Book,
used with permission.
    All quotes remain the property of the original authors and are
copyrighted in their names. Poems quoted in full are used with permission.

Library of Congress Cataloging-in-Publication Data

Corinne, Tee, 1943 –
    Dreams of the woman who loved sex.

    Bibliography: p.
    1. Lesbianism — Literary collections. I. Title.
PS3553.06474D74 1987 813'.54 87-20216
ISBN 0-934411-05-0 (pbk.)

Contents

Acknowledgments

Many people have contributed thoughts and encouragement to this book. I appreciate each and every one.

Special thanks are due the following: Carol Seajay in whose home and on whose typewriter *Dreams of the Woman Who Loved Sex* was begun; Caroline Overman, whose love and beauty provided the inspiration for the character of *Christine*; Tangren Alexander and the Southern Oregon Women Writer's Group, Gourmet Eating Society and Chorus; Ann Bannon; Georgia Cole; Barbara Wilson and Judith Barrington along with the 1986 participants in Flight of the Mind; Lonnie Barbach; Susie Bright; my uncle, Paul Hurst; Phyllis Lyon who has encouraged me in so many of my endeavors; Chris and Pat; Ben and Tom, my publishers, Bill Doody and Mary Best of Yellow Pages Bookstore and Pat Zerwer, each of whom came to my rescue, cheerfully, repeatedly; and Lee Lynch, to whom this book is dedicated, with love.

Introduction

I started writing about sexuality because I wanted stories in which I didn't have to change the pronouns and gender of the people involved; stories in which I did not feel embarrassed or offended by the actions of the characters. I wanted sexy stories that encouraged me to feel good about myself; material that would be gentle and passionate, transformative, and healing.

This book contains three distinct groups of writing. The first, "Passion Is a Forest Fire Between Us," is a first-person narrative describing an intensely sexual relationship. It is explicit, detailed, and specific, expanding outward from the main character's physical body, celebrating the senses.

The second is a suite of thirty-one poems called "The Cream Poems," one for each day in a long month. They grew out of my excitement with sexual language. I wanted to create vivid images with a minimum of words, to find the particular notations that could be a bridge between my experience and the reader's.

The final section, "Dreams of the Woman Who Loved Sex," is a multilayered text which interweaves reality, fantasy, memories, and dreams.

☆ ☆ ☆

During the years 1973–1986 I lectured on erotic art, facilitated women's sexuality groups and worked for San Francisco Sex Education Switchboard ('74–'77). I kept feeling a need for greater diversity in sex education

1

material, desiring a more inclusive range of voices, of bodies. For me this meant women's voices telling our own stories, sexuality seen through women's eyes, experiences felt through women's bodies: woman as lover as well as beloved, as actor and respondee, as viewer and person viewed. I believe that we each have our own story and that each story has an audience.

As to where my interest in sex stories came from, sometimes I claim it's because I'm a double Scorpio, the astrological sign of sex, death, and rebirth. More often I think it's because of the confusion I felt as a pre-teen and teenager trying to understand my own and others' sexual feelings and actions.

I grew up in the rural and mildly urban south, turned thirteen the same year Elvis Presley had his first hit — 1956. I saw Elvis on stage that year and felt so embarrassed that I wouldn't look, but I didn't know what was embarrassing about the scene: his movements or the crowd of cheering girls.

The summer I was twelve, I had been given a book called WHERE DO WE COME FROM which my memory says was a mechanical description of the plumbing of reproduction. Nowhere do I remember hearing about feelings, biological drives, the physical need for touching and comfort.

Although heavy censorship at the national level kept the more informative books out of this country, a relative of mine gave me Walter Benton's THIS IS MY BELOVED. It is a long, obsessive, erotic poem. THIS IS MY BELOVED filled in many of the holes in my understanding, saying that passion and love were the reason people did sexual things and saying it in a language that was warm and visceral.

I still had much to learn about sexuality but Benton's book gave me a direction in which to search, ideas to turn over, a forum for my consideration.

I read LADY CHATTERLY'S LOVER with delight when I was nineteen, STORY OF O with amazement when I was twenty-three. For a couple of years in New

2

York City, during my graduate studies in art, I read the Traveler's Companion series, hardcore pornographic paperbacks that I picked up in subway magazine stores. I thought them wildly funny and entertaining.

Somewhere in those years before my mid-twenties, I read various "how to" books, the Kinsey Report, *PSY-CHOPATHIA SEXUALIS*, and some of Havelock Ellis. Later, I read Kate Millet's *SEXUAL POLITICS* which opened up yet another world. The quotations Millet used for illustrations were terribly exciting.

MY SECRET GARDEN by Nancy Friday was a different category, a different genre: women talking candidly about their sexual fantasies. These stories felt real, were true to my own experiences, and were validating. Many of them affected me in the ways traditional erotica and pornography are supposed to—they turned me on.

Shortly after the publication of *MY SECRET GARDEN*, Anais Nin's erotic writings began appearing in book form: *DELTA OF VENUS, LITTLE BIRDS*, and *A SPY IN THE HOUSE OF LOVE*. These are very special books in which style and content merge with compelling force. I love the environments, the vivid characters, the sense of inevitability.

I realize now that I was searching for truth as well as for facts—a truth that is fuller, richer, more detailed; that encompasses motivation, biology, and destiny. Nin's writing gave all this to me.

What Nin's writing lacked was a lesbian focus.

☆ ☆ ☆

I had been finding lesbian erotica in fragments and flashes during the 1970s. I especially remember lines from Judy Grahn's poems:

"She came to me out of the silky midnight mist, her slips rustling like cow thieves," *The Psychoanalysis of Edward the Dyke.*

"She leaves the taste of salt and iron / under your tongue, but you don't mind," *Detroit Annie, Hitchhiking.*

"my lovers teeth are white geese flying above me / my lovers muscles are rope ladders under my hands," *A Woman Is Talking to Death*.

I have always treasured June Arnold's poetic description of aging and sexuality:

> Memory moved her hand to Mamie Carter's belly — skin white as milk, finely pucked like sugar-sprinkled clabber; memory dropped her hand to Mamie Carter's sparse hair curling like steel — there was strength between her legs and no dough there where the flesh was fluid enough to slip away from the bone and leave that tensed grain hard as granite and her upright violent part like an animal nose against Su's palm.
>
> *SISTER GIN*

Audre Lorde's germinal and frequently cited essay *Uses of the Erotic: The Erotic as Power*, published in 1978, broadened the perspective within which sexual energy could be understood. It also served to legitimize an interest among women in sexuality.

Lorde's prose and poetry in works such as *Tar Beach* demonstrate her gift for the artful portrayal of erotica, for theory made manifest:

> There were green plantains which we half peeled and then planted, fruit-deep, in each other's bodies until the petals of skin lay like tendrils of broad green fire upon the curly darkness between your upspread thighs. There were ripe red finger bananas, stubby and sweet, with which I parted your lips gently to insert the peeled fruit into your grape-purple flower.　*Tar Beach*

Elana Dykewomon's erotic book, *FRAGMENTS FROM LESBOS*, contains one of my all-time favorite erotic poems, one which settled into my memory with tenacity and exuberance:

> diving, i kiss and/kiss and/ kiss
> and/& kiss
> kiss/and kiss
> :underneath
> you are coral
> live red coral

Dykewomon's poem reminds me of Martha Shelley's lines: "Her Labia were like flowers, like sea anemones ... I wondered if mine were like that to her," from *Making Connections.*

And Adrienne Rich's crystalline images in *The Floating Poem, Unnumbered:* "your strong tongue and slender fingers / reaching where I had been waiting years for you / in my rose-wet cave — whatever happens, this is."

A joyous, affirming approach to woman-centered sexuality is honored also by Willyce Kim:

> ... our clits straining against the weight of bone on bone..pubic hair rubbing..wet between her fingers the soft folds as she spreads us both apart to join again and again..taking me, taking me, i want to go down on her and push my mouth up into her cunt and lover her, feel her come slide over me...close. open.
>
> *Sunday. When She Was 16. And Before Bolinas*

Sexual writing seems to convey metaphorical and allegorical meanings with ease. One example is Alicia Gaspar de Alba's poem where a description of making tortillas ends with the lines: "Tortilleras, we are called, grinders of maize, makers, bakers, / slow lovers of women. / The secret is starting from scratch." *Making Tortillas*

Kitty Tsui's series, called *Journey Poems: Red Rock Canyon, Summer 1977,* unfolds in layers of meaning. The "journey" of the title, which is also a quest, ends in a vision where spiritual and carnal knowledge are integrated:

> at the moment of climax
> i see a vision superimposed on the sky,
> i see my lover's face as she comes in my arms.
> i fall limp onto the sand.
>
> *the vision*

Realities shift repeatedly in Pearl Time'sChild's story *The Box*:

> leaving, then, this startled flesh
> this the hand, and this
> the hidden mouth and source
> wakened naked cell to cell.

And meaning enlarges suddenly in *Sides* by Margaret Sloan-Hunter: "tensions exploding / as you wet my face / with your trust."

Canadian lesbians, both francophone and anglophone, have contributed their own complex, rich, dense writings which often incorporate a formal erotization of language itself. Nicole Brossard, Daphne Marlatt and Betsy Warland share with French author Monique Wittig, author of *THE LESBIAN BODY*, an exploratory approach to language; dislocating and reassembling words and ideas into patterns of meaning that are often associative rather than linear.

For instance, Nicole Brossard, writer, editor, and publisher from Quebec, writes:

> Fictive theory: words were used only in the ultimate embrace. The first word lips and sticky saliva on her breasts. Theory begins there when the breast or the child moves away.
>
> THESE OUR MOTHERS, B. Godard, trans.

Daphne Marlatt, a British Columbian writer and co-founder of the dynamic, bilingual literary magazine *TESSERA* writes:

> ... terra incognita known, *geysa*, gush, upwelling in the hidden Norse we found, we feel it thrust as waters part for us, hot, through fern, frost, volcanic thrust. it's all there, love, we part each other coming to, geyser, sprouting pool, hidden in and under separate skin we make for each other through.
>
> in the dark of the coast

U.S. born Canadian writer Betsy Warland, a founding editor of *(f)LIP*, a feminist innovative writing news-letter, writes in V from *OPEN IS BROKEN:*

> bodies joined north and south
> we are each other's entrance
> kissing vulva lips
> tongues torque way into vortex
> leave syllables behind

Equally powerful, yet very different, are the words of the U.S. born Canadian writer Jane Rule when she writes, in *Lilian*, of a woman who "likes to come first . . . quickly, in disarray, one exposed breast at your mouth, your hand beneath trousers pulled down only low enough to reveal the mound of curly red-gold hair."

I can't remember when I first read the English author Mary Renault's *THE MIDDLE MIST*, but many images in it entered into my fantasy life, especially passages involving the androgynous Leo. Renault's first novel, *PROMISE OF LOVE* (1939), also contains a memorable lesbian in the person of Colonna, a nurse:

> She wore, as she always did, man-tailored clothes of a cut that would have looked flamboyant on a man, but which she succeeded somehow in subduing to her personality . . . While she removed them with the speed acquired in hospital she contrived to make love to Vivian tacitly, expertly, and with the finesse that made it the merest running commentary to the conversation.

Renault's Colonna is an archetypal figure, sharing qualities of erotic excitement with Radclyffe Hall's Stephen Gordon, with Ann Bannon's Beebo Brinker and with Gale Wilhelm's Jan Morale. All are stylized, ambi-gendered figures possessing charismatic personal charm. Each has a place in my heart and in my waking dreams.

Sexuality is a subject matter that can easily be trivialized by humor, yet humor can also lighten tensions, make difficult material accessible. Chocolate Waters, Marilyn Gayle and SDiane Bogus all have the gift of writing humorously about sexuality without demeaning their subject.

In *Dyke Hands*, for instance, SDiane Bogus takes a fresh and refreshing look at sex organs:

> Because dyke hands are the sexual organs of lesbian love, they can be as shocking to view as the penis through an open fly, or as bold (delicious) to behold as the breast of a woman suddenly uncovered.

Later in the same irreverent piece she notes:

> Not all dykes are teasers, as such, but you can bet if they have dyke hands, and they are brought forth, they seem to appear at the end of their wrists the split second before you are touched.

Self-sexuality has been an issue of female emancipation at least since 1974 when Betty Dodson published *LIBERATING MASTURBATION*. Dodson's book, with its enthusiastic text and accompanying line drawings of women's genitals, was an instant consciousness-raiser.

Lesbian writers have explored masturbation in a variety of ways. Becky Birtha treats it like a healthy meal or refreshing shower in *The Gray Whelk Shell*: "She lets it happen slowly, rise to fullness, lets it flush her like a warm, salt tide."

Martha Courtot infuses it with transcendence in *Making Love to Myself*: "my body is a bird / hovering / just above the sand / and sea; it moves with the tide / out and in / wave after wave / bringing myself / home to myself / i come, and i come, and i come."

In *Erotica*, claire indigo combines self-loving with seduction:

> she was always with her fingers in her cunt, that one. i would see her sitting in her chair reading, her fingers between her folds. she would take them and place them in her mouth. or sitting on the bed talking together her fingers would rise to her nose, her lips. she would lick them or seeing me watch her she would smile or laugh devilishly and raise her fingers to my lips . . ."

And then there's the aftermath of sex when hours

or days later it all comes back as in *After* by Valerie
Taylor, quoted in full:

> Impossible to get closer
> than the smell of you on my hand
> after the bed is made,
> towels tossed in the hamper.
> Moving around the kitchen
> sniff
> remembered excitement.

There are many other treasured lines, poems, stories,
like Ann Allen Shockley's forest imagery in *LOVING HER*
or the older women making love in an apple orchard
in Valerie Taylor's *PRISM*. There is a wealth of lesbian
erotic material, scattered, rewarding the active searcher,
the responsive reader.

I have chosen some of those that lodged in my
memory, writings to which I responded strongly, where
the prose dissolved leaving me with an afterglow of
images and feelings.

☆ ☆ ☆

In 1973 I heard Betty Dodson lecture on self-loving.
After the lecture I told her I wanted to do drawings of
women's genitals. "Aw, do it, honey," was her response,
delivered in a disarming midwestern drawl.

I did. The drawings were published in 1975 as the
CUNT COLORING BOOK, reprinted by Naiad Press in
1981 as *LABIAFLOWERS*.

Following the coloring book, I made photographs
of women's genitals and a slide – animation called
SAPPHOCENTRIC LOVE STORY in which two rag dolls
make love.

In 1975 I began photographing women making love.
One of my photos was used as the cover for a magazine
called *SINISTER WISDOM*. This image was subsequently
distributed as a poster. Other of my photographs appeared
in *THE SEX ATLAS, COUNTRY WOMEN'S POETRY*, and
YELLOW SILK.

With each new picture, I was visually exploring
taboos, making a type of image that I hadn't seen before.

I was fascinated and passionately absorbed by this work. In 1982, Naiad Press published a book of my erotic photographs combined with Jacqueline Lapidus's poetry. The book's title, YANTRAS OF WOMANLOVE, refers to the visual corollary to mantras: yantras are diagrams of energy.

Around 1978, I took photographs of a woman in a wheelchair kissing her able-bodied lover. These images have appeared in A WOMAN'S TOUCH, SAPPHIC TOUCH, HERESIES' sex issue, Off Our Backs" disability issue and the 1984 edition of OUR BODIES/ OURSELVES.

And then, after ten years of work in the art of sexual imagery, I began writing. One craft did not exclude, but rather seemed to complement the other.

I began writing erotica in 1984 while recovering from surgery. Lonnie Barbach was offering $1000 for erotic short stories. I'd fantasied about writing sexy stories. Now, motivated by medical bills as well as dreams, I settled into the writing. I loved the process.

My stories are in both of Lonnie Barbach's anthologies, PLEASURES, Women Write Erotica and EROTIC INTERLUDES, Tales Told by Women, and in the magazines ON OUR BACKS and YONI.

I feel privileged to live at this time in history and to work in such a fertile and expanding field.

The Women-In-Print movement (that is, women publishing books and magazines, women's bookstores, printers, and distributors) has made both an ideological and a financial change in the nature of women's erotica. Literature, ideas, and visual art have been reproduced and spread around the world. The information that is available now is very different from what was there even fifteen years ago.

Several books produced by women's presses have been important and influential to me. Many contain my artwork. The most significant are: A WOMAN'S TOUCH, Nelly and Cedar, eds.; I AM MY LOVER, Blank and Cottrell; *LOVING WOMEN*, the Nomadic Sisters; *SAP-PHISTRY*, Califia; and *LESBIAN SEX*, Loulan.

Many of the Women's Movement magazines have produced special issues on sexuality. Some of these are rhetorical or political: dealing with sex in a generalized, distanced, didactic manner. Others, like *COUNTRY WOMEN*, exhibit a remarkable gutsiness and candor.

In the mid-1980s a new type of magazine appeared within the Women's Movement: the lesbian sex magazine. Openly iconoclastic, often confrontive, magazines like *ON OUR BACKS*, *BAD ATTITUDE*, and *YONI* have redefined the dialectic of sexuality within lesbian-feminism. They have done this by giving body, form and vision to the discussions generated by theorists like Amber Hollibaugh and Cherríe Moraga and by conferences like Feminist Perspectives on Pornography (1978, San Francisco) and the Barnard Conference on Women and Sexuality (1982, N.Y.C.).

The magazines, various books and pamphlets, and a variety of public presentations, have generated controversy and, at times, discord. What seems clearest to me is that I prefer the richness of the present to the silence of the past.

Bibliography

June Arnold, *SISTER GIN* (Plainfield, VT: Daughters, Ind., 1975).

Becky Birtha, "The Gray Whelk Shell," *COMMON LIVES/ LESBIAN LIVES* (No. 6, Winter 1982).

SDiane Bogus, "Dyke Hands," *COMMON LIVES/LESBIAN LIVES* (No. 5, Fall 1982).

Nicole Brossard, *THESE OUR MOTHERS*, trans. Barbara Godard (Quebec: Coach House Quebec Translations, 1983).

Martha Courtot, *TRIBE* (San Francisco: Pearlchild, 1976).

Elana Dykewomon, *FRAGMENTS FROM LESBOS* (Langlois, OR: Diaspora, 1981).

Alicia Gaspar de Alba, "Making Tortillas," *COMMON LIVES/LESBIAN LIVES* (No. 20, Summer 1986).

Marilyn Gayle and Barbary Katherine, *WHAT LESBIANS DO* (Portland, OR: Godiva, 1975).

Judy Grahn, *THE WORK OF A COMMON WOMAN* (Oakland, CA: Diana Press, 1978).

Amber Hillibaugh and Cherrie Moraga, "What We're Rolling Around in Bed With: Sexual Silences in Feminism," *POWERS OF DESIRE*, edited by Snitow, Stansell, and Thompson (NY: Monthly Review Press, 1983).

claire indigo, "erotica," *COMMON LIVES/LESBIAN LIVES* (No. 10, Winter 1983).

Willyce Kim, *UNDER THE ROLLING SKY* (Oakland, CA: Maud Gonne Press, 1976).

Audre Lorde, "Tar Beach," *CONDITIONS: FIVE* (Vol. II, No. 2, Autumn 1979).

Daphne Marlatt, *TOUCH TO MY TONGUE* (Edmonton, Alberta: Longspoon Press, 1984).

Adrienne Rich, *THE DREAM OF A COMMON LANGUAGE* (NY: W. W. Norton & Co., 1978).

Jane Rule, *OUTLANDER* (Tallahassee, FL: The Naiad Press, Inc., 1981).

Martha Shelley, *CROSSING THE DMZ* (Oakland, CA: The Womens Press Collective, 1974).

Ann Allen Shockley, *LOVING HER* (Indianapolis, IN: Bobbs-Merrill, 1974).

Margaret Sloan-Hunter, "Sides," *YONI* (Vol. 1, Autumn 1986).

Valerie Taylor, *TWO WOMEN: The Poetry of Jeannette Foster and Valerie Taylor* (Chicago: Womanpress, 1986).

———, *PRISM* (Tallahassee, FL: The Naiad Press, Inc., 1981).

Pearl Time'sChild, "The Box," *A WOMAN'S TOUCH* edited by Cedar and Nelly (Grants Pass, OR: Womanshare Books, 1979).

Kitty Tsui, *THE WORDS OF A WOMAN WHO BREATHES FIRE* (San Francisco: Spinsters, Ink, 1983).

Betsy Warland, *OPEN IS BROKEN* (Edmonton, Alberta: Longspoon Press, 1984).

Chocolate Waters, *TAKE ME LIKE A PHOTOGRAPH* (Denver, CO: Eggplant Press, 1977).

Passion Is A
Forest Fire Between Us

Part I:

Seeds

Of course that all ended long ago. It's been years since I've thought of her with any frequency. But, Oh God, it was sweet while it lasted.

April

I'm driving north from San Francisco through the central valley, filled with acres of rice plants, almond trees, past Shasta the Magnificent, well into the forested Cascades. This is the year I'll turn thirty-eight. A restlessness is upon me. The winter has been arduous, spring inside me a long time coming. I wear a gardenia for perfume and luck.

I've traveled this segment of the I-5 corridor three times before, once with my former husband and twice with lovers, Leah and Maggie. Each trip has formed a dividing line, marking a change in my life, in who I am in the world. I feel myself open, searching.

I spend the night in a motel outside a small, mountainous, river town; wake to masturbate, shower, eat and shop for gift food for my friends. My period starts just before I check out of the motel. Slow rain begins as I leave the interstate and wind along progressively deteriorating back roads, ease through clay-lined potholes, weave around rain-cut gullies.

15

I arrive to warm greetings, laughter, tea, hot stones wrapped in cloth to ease my cramps. We talk for hours. My friends have a quiet, intense woman my age living in a cabin on their land, helping with the chores. Her name is Christine. Although I'm interested in getting to know her better, my cramps begin to disorient me. I spend the afternoon in bed, reading and sleeping.

During the evening meal I am constantly aware of Christine's presence. I sense her watching me although she never seems to be when I actually look at her. We clean the dishes side by side, our hands and arms brushing as we pass and dry the pots, bowls, mugs, utensils. Time elongates. She smells faintly of wood smoke, reaches to squeeze my hand briefly when we finish.

As a group we gather to meditate on healing, hold hands, focusing, sitting quietly in the twilight, a single candle burning. Christine's hand is warm in mine, her leg warm against my own. Her presence seems to roll across my body in a hot flood of sensation. Desire clogs my throat. I want to look at her, search for a sign that this experience is mutual. At the same time, I covet the privateness of my experience, claim it possessively, don't open my eyes or turn, fearing to interrupt the energy building toward its own peak as I arch inwardly, hold my breath as pleasure ripples up and down my spine.

The circle breaks. Christine leans to kiss my cheek and leaves for the night. My friends and I talk awhile before I climb into my sleeping loft to sort and savor these new developments in my life. I have so many questions for her, about her; so many threads unraveling at once.

In the morning, after breakfast, I volunteer to help Christine gather rocks to fill holes in the road. Later we sit on the tailgate of her truck talking about our lives with an ease and comfort that astounds me. I feel as if I've always known her, as if we are renewing rather than beginning a friendship.

Returning to the main house, my cramps begin again. Christine offers to give me a back rub. I've never known a touch like hers before. Melting into her fingers, my pain dissolves in a wash of sensuality.

"Will you join me in my cabin, after dinner?" she asks, husky voiced, breathy.

"Oh, yes," I answer, squeezing her hand in assent, in affirmation.

Working near her in the afternoon I vibrate to her presence. When the others briefly leave us alone, we touch, then cling to each other. In the doorway to a building, she presses hard against me; my nipples feel the weave of my shirt, the pounding of both our hearts. Blood rushes to my head. Intense, this deep-rooted, intuitive response.

Too soon we must rejoin the others, help with dinner, socialize.

"So you're spending the night with Christine?" one friend says, knowingly. I wonder when she told them, learn that she didn't: the electricity between us was, quite simply, visible.

We climb the dark hill to her cabin, build a fire in the stove, drink hot chocolate, maneuver into the cozy sleeping loft. I quickly undress, stretch and wait. She joins me and I feel a sense of homecoming: the combining of two entities, long separated. Slowly she lowers her torso on top of mine, responding to my slightest move, pressing, rubbing. Passion is a wave, a forest fire between us, spreading, enveloping. I reach over her hip and engage her labia from behind, seeking out her clitoris, her central cone of power. She wiggles up to meet my hand, show me how to please her. I explore all her openings, touch her from both sides, wanting to know her boundaries, wanting to give her joy. Her pleasure is long and evident although she doesn't come.

Rolling to my side, she kisses and kneads my breasts. Usually my nipples are more sensitive, my breasts less so. In her deft, small, powerful hands the whole expanse

17

of my flesh seems to awaken and greet her, push outward to eliminate the distance between us. Kneeling, she massages my rib cage, my belly, leaving watery muscles, tingling nerves in her wake. Her fingers comb through my pubic hair, graze my crest and swollen, hidden lips. She licks her fingers and separates my layers, kneeling now between my legs, watching my response. Excitement radiates from my body: desire unbound. She drops to kiss and lick between my legs. I tense, worrying that I haven't bathed adequately these past two days. Sensing my withdrawal, she tells me that I taste sweet, smell fine. I put aside my personal squeamishness and flow again toward her, welcoming her.

No one before has touched my body with such familiarity, drawn from me such a spectrum of delight. Her lips and fingers slide inside me, wrap around me, lay my spirit bare. I am filled with wonder, awe; humbled. I reach out for her with my psyche as well as my loins, knowing the stirrings of a warm, new hunger.

Patiently she continues, dissolving my barriers, inciting my nerves to riot. My orgasm builds like an immense structure. My flesh expands to contain it. I come with a rushing, falling feeling, merging with her.

After, she tells me that she never comes the first time with someone new. Usually I come easily, indiscriminately, high on the excitement of a first encounter. We seem so different in the details of our yearly lives, feel to me so similar inside. Wrapped in her arms, legs entwined, I sleep deeply, do not remember dreaming.

Morning enters through the skylight above my face. She's awake already, watching me. Memories of the night before overwhelm me. She questions me about my expectations, my predilection for one-night stands.

"This is not a casual relationship," I inform her, sitting up.

"I love you," she says, then looks surprised, starts to apologize.

I reassure her, tell her I could have been the one to say it, so full of loving her I feel.

We make love again and this time she does come, unmistakably, gratifyingly. In the afterglow I tell her I'm glad that I can trust in what she says.

Blissfully, I drift through breakfast of cold toast and warm coffee, touch her with my eyes and hands. I float through the day. We embrace spontaneously and often, long for privacy and time. I change my travel plans, arrange to stay another day before my city job calls me back. I find it hard to remember that we met three days before.

☆ ☆ ☆

I drive south, past the holy mountain, volcanic, snow-capped. Wild irises cluster along the embankments. An hour from the city which has been my primary relationship for the past seven years, I begin a hallucinatory dialogue with my dead grandfather. In it I tell him about Christine, how shaken I am by her, the abruptness and depth of my feeling. I tell him I want to return, spend more time with her, explore potential futures. He encourages me, says my thinking seems sound and reasonable.

Arriving home I'm restless, walk around the neighborhood, buy myself some peonies. Late into the twilight I sit, drawing the rich white blossoms. I go out for Chinese food, return to work on an illustration for a friend's poem. At four a.m. I finally go to bed. A few days later a letter, accompanied by a poem, arrives in the mail from Christine:

> I still, after all these years, do not understand desire —
> The fire that blossoms in April rain . . .
>
> Wrenched suddenly into the sweetness of another
> spring
> I find that beneath the pure and dazzling clarity of
> winter's snow
> My roots have grown
>
> In a blaze of mingled terror and delight
> My whole body, beating hotly,
> Clenches and unclenches its single, secret bud.
>
> Exuberantly, Christine

How pleased I am that the passion that birthed my recent drawings has stirred her creativity as well. She tells me it is the first poem she has written in five years.

Her letters are charming, urbane, witty, sometimes self-mocking, brimming with quotes and references. I read and reread them, ferreting out different levels of meaning.

I call my Aunt Ruth and tell her I am in love. I describe Christine in detail (yes, withholding some), stress her academic accomplishments (a classics scholar, PhD), dwell on our similarities. Ruth is supportive, encouraging. I tell her about my conversations with my grandfather. She says he is a good person to seek counsel from, always had a sound head on his shoulders.

My doctor phones. The pap smear she took recently has returned from the lab a class three. She tells me that my cervix is precancerous and must be watched carefully, wants me to come in for another examination immediately.

All this I write to Christine. She responds that she is sending me healing energy each evening at 8 p.m. One evening I sit in the dark of my living room, the peonies beside me, one candle burning. I hold out my hands seeking Chris and our friends together in their own twilight. A circle of seated figures shimmers briefly and dissolves around me. I feel affirmed.

The second smear comes back a class two. The doctor explains that this is an improvement, will wait three months and make another test. Sometimes, she says, these conditions heal themselves.

Christine writes again, discusses physics, Durrell's *ALEXANDRIA QUARTET*, photography, perception. She signs her letter "I hold you in my thoughts."

May

I return to spend five days with Christine after three weeks in the city. She comes racing down the hill to meet me, grinning, swinging me in circles. I feel slow and sluggish after eight hours on the road, am over-whelmed and dizzied by her response, feel shy and awk-ward. She beams at me anyway, helps carry my belong-ings to her cabin.

She shows me a small apple tree she has transplanted near her porch. She's named it Korinna after a Greek poet whose work reminds her of me. One blossom raises fragile petals to us from a delicate limb.

I've brought poetry to share with her, a manuscript of Martha Courtot's recent work. She hands me a copy of Chocolate Waters' TAKE ME LIKE A PHOTOGRAPH, a favorite book of mine. I admire the new bed she has built against the wall on the main floor of her cabin, tucked neatly under the ladder to the loft. She has the evening free to spend with me in the cabin if we choose to stay and not join the others.

I choose to stay.

We settle into the new bed, our backs supported by a broad sofa pillow propped against the shelf that runs along one wall. I tell her about my imaginary conversations with my dead grandfather, too aberrant seeming for me to communicate in a letter. She tells me about missing me, about subatomic particles, and Hei-senberg's Principle of Indeterminacy. Late afternoon sun

21

slants through the windows, highlighting dust in the air. The room is golden.

I open Water's book and start to read aloud: "She comes to me at night / Her tongue glistening / Her body tuned / . . . Gently I will play her / Favorite song and Sing to her in tongues / When she comes / To me / At night." (*She*) And later: "Your body's full of openings and closings . . . Your legs spread wide and open / Opening and closing / my mouth inside and open / wide . . ." (*Openings and Closings*).

Later still I read:

> I wanna come all over ya
> Wanna put my face inside yer mouth
> Wanna put my mouth inside yer legs
> Want yer face all over me
> Willya lemme?
> Willya open up yer legs?
> Lemme tell ya that I love yer legs?
> 'Specially when they're open
> List'ning to my mouth
> List'ning to my lips / My tongue against ya
> Didja know I love ya?
> Love the way ya smell
> Wanna smell ya
> Wanna taste ya
> Wanna eat ya
> Wanna love ya
> Willya lemme?
> Willya come?
> Willya come all over me?
> If ya do I'll love ya
> If ya do I'll letcha
> Jesus willya lemme?
> Jesus willya lemme?

(I Wanna)

Not particularly politically correct by lesbian community standards but quite evocative and, well yes, quite stimulating. She has been gently moulding my breasts as I read, now she slides one leg over mine and begins to tug at the fastening of my pants. She seems to think I can go on reading despite her skillful attentions. I put the book aside and grin at her, shaking my head no. Laughingly she pulls my pants and briefs off, begins to lick my labia. I feel enchanted, the poetry still lively in the room, her light-touched head disappearing behind my dark curls. Heavenly woman, how fortunate I feel, how blessed.

She thrusts her tongue deep inside me, drawing the honey out, my soft golden bear. I close my eyes, smiling, and send my awareness down to touch her from the inside, noting how big my clitoris is, how turgid the inner lips. She breathes warm air on me and enters me with one, maybe two, fingers. I expand, tent out, my uterus moves up and back. I feel her move around inside me, slickly brush the walls. I know you, woman, I say to her silently, rising to her ministrations. "I know you, woman, and I will know you better," I whisper, loving her.

She strokes my tummy, brings her finger down to press my small, swollen rod within its protective covering. I cry out with pleasure, make little short hums with each exhalation, roll my head against my neck, turtle into my shoulders. She accelerates, I follow. My breathing is rough, fingers and toes drawn into spasms. I clench my teeth, bear down with my abdominal muscles, upper arms gripping my ribs, shoulders down and pushing harder. I come, my breath snorting out, arms wrapped tight around myself; my shoulders toss from side to side.

I'm shivering after the violence of my conclusion. She covers me with her body. Her mouth seeks mine, proprietary. I breathe deeply of my own smell, still clinging to her face. When I reach for her, I find her nether regions swampy, inviting. I finger her pearl caught between our bodies, savor the liquid of our loving. She starts to shake in all her limbs, teeth chattering against

23

mine, knees and toes banging. "I think I'd better turn over," she says with several catches in her voice. We rearrange our bodies and I begin again, pressing, kneading. "Here? Here?"

"Oh, yes," she says. "Don't stop. Please don't stop."

I have no intention of stopping, coax her onward, slide my fingers in large ovals around her vestibule. The opening to her vagina contracts as I circle, the spasms small, preparatory.

I rub her shaft between two fingers in long sweeps, following the creases.

"Yes. Yes," she says. "That's it," she says. "I'm coming."

This last trails off as the large spasms take her body. I continue rubbing, following her as she crests and ebbs, comforting her as she releases back into the present. She turns her face into my shoulder and breathes in long sighing heaves.

"I like the way you do that," she says.

"I like the way you come," I tell her. "Oh, Christine, I do like the way you come."

☆ ☆ ☆

Sunlight floods my body. She and I burst through the cabin door with only one hour's privacy before we have to join the group again. I press myself to her body, sliding up and down against her. She touches me lightly, shoulders, face, neck, hair. Our lips brush and hold. I am radiating outward, becoming part of the light-filled trees, shimmering leaves, dazzling heat beyond. I hear our breathing from far away, sense her urgency, my own, gaining strength, drawing my attention back into my body.

She tears at my cutoffs, reaches inside to touch the physical roots of my passion, further to the inner ocean that swells and laps at her fingers. Those fingers dive repeatedly into my center and I push to meet them, long to melt into them, lose my edges. I lean my forehead into her shoulder, smell the fresh tart-sweetness of her

24

excitement, feel tears cover my eyes, spill across my cheeks, her shirt.

My legs will no longer support my weight so I back up to her desk and rest on the edge of it. "Oh, god," I cry quietly. Then louder, "Oh, god," and hear my voice almost a sob and wish I could tell her how magical I feel, awash with sensation, adoring her for bringing me here again.

My body bunches, curves. She arches in sympathy with me. My fingers wrap into balls, fists, beat gently against her back and shoulders. Her fingers increase their demanding plunges, sounds of water caught and pushed aside.

I submerge in a whirlpool. Sensations ripple over all my surfaces, call forth a response along my bones. My swirling vortex centers on her hand between my legs, expands, implodes, sends me spinning in waves outward, crying out loudly to her in my ancient pleasure. The sound is one long sustained note like the call of a conch horn, falling off finally, trailing away like my tears, ending in sobs bubbling from deep inside—cleansing, freeing tears.

"Oh, Christine, oh, Christine. Who are you? How can you . . . ?" I touch her face with wonder. She kisses me, anchors me in this world, this room. I match my breathing to hers, relax, space out, return clear-eyed, clear-headed, firmly here, thankful for her presence in my life.

☆ ☆ ☆

One night, lying in bed all soft from loving, I tell her I want to propose to her, want to make plans for a future together. I know that she has other lovers living elsewhere but think the fire in her must surely match my own. She tells me she has promised someone else that she will go and live with her, help her homestead in the far north. At first I argue with her, I plead, we fight. I tell her this other affair is transitory, will end, can't possibly match what happens between us. She calls me arrogant. I tell her she's a dummy and a fool. I shake her when I tell her this, then cry and finally walk alone in the moonlight. I return calm but grieve inside.

The next morning she is contrite, starts to cry after breakfast, pained at having hurt me. I tease her into stopping, telling her our friends will think she's the injured party, instead of me. The following day I leave. I've told her I need to know when I will see her again. I will return in August. I hope she will join me then.

Two weeks later she calls, just as I'm preparing to leave for the East Coast. She has decided to join me in August. I sense undertones of leaving the other woman but nothing is said. Part of me is pleased, but the hurt child in me still cries. A few weeks later I write her not to come, that I don't want to see her then after all. I determine to put her memory out of my mind, the pain too great. I won't allow her to hurt me like that again.

July

A year has passed since Christine entered and left my life so abruptly. Although I dream about her and think of her sometimes with longing, I love my city life, my job, my friends. There is comfort here, and security. And who knows when some exciting, devastatingly attractive woman will walk into my life? I know she exists just around every corner, in every restaurant, at every meeting, in every smile.

I return to the mountains to teach a summer course and find Christine waiting when I arrive.

I feel her like a physical shock in all my parts. She has lived her pioneering dream and has now returned to our friends' land to teach and write and edit, filling in with whatever needs to be done.

She tells me that she grieved over losing me, wondered where and how I was.

The first week I keep Christine at a distance. We take the time to talk, to become friends, a process our original passion had bypassed. I enjoy her company and conversation. Evenings we walk the back roads, pass fields of daisies, red paintbrush, St. John's wort. Dried madrone leaves rattle, giving summer a touch of autumn nostalgia. We talk about aesthetics, Andre Malraux, Judy Chicago. I twine my arm through hers.

She acknowledges that our original attraction had been more than merely physical, adding, "I would do it again for the sex alone." I am shaken, torn between

27

my conflicting desires for security and abandon. In the early hours of the following day, I decide to give in to my longings, become lovers with her again. I'm willing to take the consequences, want the healing her presence brings into my life.

I tell her this after the evening program ends, learn she's loaned her cabin to another couple for the night, plans on sleeping out to give them privacy. Suddenly, we're like teenagers with no place to go. We wander about saying goodnight to various groups, hugging others, each other.

As she prepares her sleeping bag, removes her outer garments, she seems even more desirable. She begs me to touch her and I do, weaving my hand through the layers to her hidden valley. We lie together in the moonlight until I become chilled, return to sleep in my own bed.

I have the following afternoon free and we meet at her cabin, not wanting to tell the others yet what we are doing. Alone together, time collapses, the year we spent apart seems to disappear. Our lovemaking is wild and gentle by turns.

The first time I come again in her hands, I burst into tears that tear at me, seem to have no bottom. I mourn the time we spent apart. She reads sections from her northern journal, passages that mention me, dreams she had about me, times she grieved. We cry together, console each other, make love again. Outside, in the midst of this normally dry season, rain comes down.

August

I am sitting in a Japanese restaurant, thinking about Christine, eating sashimi. I hold the pieces of raw tuna in my mouth, press them with my tongue, remembering. The saké wine is elegant in its long-stemmed glass, will not overpower my body the way saké itself does.

I imagine I'm having dinner with her (when I'm not imagining that I'm eating her). There are, in my mind, two glasses of wine on the small, lacquered table, two graceful plates of sashimi, two bowls of rice. Perhaps we have just seen an afternoon movie, or maybe we will go to the theater tonight.

I am courting her with poetry, quoting Yosano Akiko's words:

> I can give myself to her
> In her dreams
> Whispering her own poems
> In her ear as she sleeps beside me.

In truth I wish I could sleep beside her again, wake up in her arms, embarrassed by the spittle on her shoulder. But she is far away and I am alone in this pristine, exciting city. Dreaming of her, I press more fish flesh in my mouth, suck the juices, inhale as the green horseradish warms my throat.

I order green tea ice cream, more wine, twirl the liquid in my glass. Koto music plays like the sounds of a stream at the edge of my awareness. I let it in and follow the melody, wondering if she likes concerts. Does she in fact enjoy music at all? I think back. Yes, she told me she played Linda Ronstadt records during the year in the north, letting them evoke memories of riding with me, playing country and western tapes on the cassette in my car. Will she like the koto music I often play while working, like raw fish and red bean pastries? Will we ever spend time together, learning each other's ways?

I pay my bill and leave, carrying a fleeting sense of her presence. The ginkgo leaves I pass seem to heighten my longing, with their shapes like exotic, exaggerated tears. I remember one of Yamakawa Tomiko's poems, answering her lover Akiko, where she laments:

> The white roses I tried to braid in my hair
> have all fallen
> around my pillow of sickness.

My pillow is one of sadness. Yearning for Christine I walk the streets willing her to appear from around every corner. She was not nearly so hard to leave a year ago, after she had chosen to go off with someone else.

Returning to my empty apartment, I decide to masturbate, place lighted candles in the bathroom, burn incense, shower, then switch the flow to the faucet, lower my body under the gently running water, caress myself and remember.

September

My life has become a roller coaster ride. Regularly, letters arrive from Christine; thoughtful, news-filled letters. Their content is quite ordinary, their effect on me profound.

Today I'm sitting in the back room of my local women's bookstore, a favorite retreat, rereading the final lines Christine has written. "I keep thinking my answer would be different if you ever make a proposal to me again. I suppose at the moment it is not too late, only too soon. But I will wait for you. And, yes, this is a proposal."

The letter both frightens and excites me. I feel as if my soul yearns for her, my intelligence warns, "Beware." I will see her briefly next month, then stay for several weeks in March when we will organize a magazine. I tell myself to proceed with caution yet carry this letter inside my coat, read and reread it as autumn takes the city.

October

I have managed to schedule three days with Christine into an intense lecture tour. I arrive exhausted, my period just ending. Our friends organize meetings to discuss the magazine project which begins in March. Christine and I have very little time alone and most of that I sleep, grateful for her protective arms.

On the third day we take time for ourselves, rest, talk, heal. Wrapped in her arms, the cabin warm, my body finally begins to unclench. Christine soothes me, strokes my back, rubs my neck. The months preceding this visit have worn me out, stretched me thin and wraithlike inside. Now my spirit takes on flesh again, expands, spreads.

She kisses me, oh soft woman's lips, closed, pressing in upon me; downy woman's cheek, flesh both firm and pliant. Her tongue slips slowly just inside the boundary of my mouth, touching and withdrawing. I suck her in, squeeze, engage. She moves in further, retreats, caresses the inside of my gums, unfolds the labyrinth of my desire. Please let me deserve this woman, I think, not for the first time.

I arch against her, strain against our clothes, my skin. She moves to cover me, rubs against my breast, secures my psyche. I unbutton her shirt, rub against her breasts; tender, heavy, ripe, rose petal smooth, pale. I slide my hands along them, pull them against my face, suckle, squeeze her thigh between my legs.

I slip down into another level of comfort, pulling her to me, burying my face in her marshmallow softness, moulding her supple, yielding body with my hands. Pulling back, she swings her breasts against my face, banging it with dull thuds, talcum powder, dusty, encompassing. My own nipples are erect and aching, my clitoris a burning coal, my breathing sharp, uneven. I take her in my mouth again, push my breasts against her hands, her fingers. Fire-laced rivers reach toward my cunt.

Unfastening my pants, she parts my hair and gently kneads my mons, fingers my clit. My breathing changes, smooths as I move to follow this new pattern, note the delicacy of her loving, release another level of tension. I struggle out of my clothes, help her out of hers. The cold wind outside drops an octave, becomes a warm wind rushing through my body, lifting me to meet her.

She spreads the hairs again, the inner lips. Her kisses, like butterfly touches, become demanding. I pull her around so I can touch and kiss her, there, between her legs, surrounded by her softness, her smells. Outside, the wind has whipped the trees into a frenzy, wailing and moaning. Inside my hot wind spreads throughout my body, moves in nerve-tingling gusts. I lick her with abandon. Her tongue invades my privacy, assaults my final barriers, speaks to the child in me, welcomes her, reassures her. I yield with an outflowing of emotion, coming hard, pushing out, shaking. She follows soon after, a small gale, a hurricane.

Returning to my side, we rest against each other, build the fire again, drink cocoa. I feel too full of her for words, feel her inside as well as out. Loving.

For weeks after this encounter I feel restless, inward. Everything that had seemed so satisfying before has now become barren, empty, binding. I want Christine yet fear the intensity of our encounters. Listening to myself tell an old friend about my present life I hear the words unhappy, difficult, troubled, struggle. I think I should do something to clear my vision, lift my spirit, but am unsure of the best course of action. Any movement at all seems more than I can manage.

I look for signs, some indication of what to do, how to reorganize my life so that I feel whole again. The wind is blowing, the sun comes out and disappears.

One evening I set out candles representing the powerful women in my past, burn incense for the child I once was. I fill a goblet with cider in thankfulness for nurturance, the gift my grandfather gave me. I put river-smoothed stones on the table: a light stone that looks like a woman's ass, a dark stone — smooth and cold.

I take the Tarot deck from its purple velvet sack, choose the love card, the two of cups, to represent me. I shuffle the cards slowly, asking for a vision of the future, laugh out loud when I turn the "Joy" card over in the position representing present forces. It shows a child being held by an adult while a ship sails off in the distance. I wonder if "Joy" means losing some pleasures in order to embrace others?

My hopes and fears are represented by the "Birth" card, my roots by the "Sun" card. Finally, I turn the Ace of Cups, a celebratory card, here representing obstacles.

I do a second reading to clarify the first and come away from it with the following: wisdom takes cultivation, ambition can be scrutinized more closely before it leads to overwhelming pressures. Grow.

I put the cards away, clear the table feeling thoughtful, momentarily calmed.

☆ ☆ ☆

In December, Christine is required, temporarily, to leave the communal land where she lives. She chooses to travel north, to visit her family and several past lovers. I wonder if she'll sleep with any of them? All of them?

The rain is cold, falls incessantly. The heat in my building is inadequate to warm me. Fog horns moan at all hours.

Decembers are usually difficult for me. This one seems interminable.

Part II:

Blossoms

March

Christine stands behind the airport glass, beaming her pleasure at my return, waiting to greet me, to hold me. I am so glad to be here. My destiny and choices seem close to converging.

She holds my hand as she drives, shy at first then spilling over with words. I begin to relax.

Safe in her cabin we undress and lie together, warming each other, becoming reacquainted. Her schedule here has altered, allowing her more time to write. She eats supper in her cabin now instead of with the larger group, has prepared a stew for my homecoming. We light a lantern and candle against the dusk, eat in companionable silence; our comfort with each other grows again.

We discuss an article about violence between lovers which she has just had published. She has been worried that I wouldn't like it. I am impressed by her honesty and thoughtfulness, the grace of her prose.

We touch and talk for hours, bringing together the details of our separate lives, the thoughts that wouldn't fit in letters, our need to be physically assured of the other's presence, attention.

Her hands and voice move over me. I reach for her, strain against her. When, much later, we finally choose to come, my orgasm is like a sigh, gentle and deeply satisfying, hers is like a subterranean movement of the earth.

☆ ☆ ☆

The magazine work proceeds at an erratic pace, sometimes smoothly, sometimes a jumble of complexities and
conflicting goals. The energy flowing between Christine
and me soothes my nerves. Our lovemaking releases tensions and creativity.

One afternoon we take our blanket and sandwiches
and climb, half sliding, down the embankment, cross
the stream and follow an old logging trail until we reach
the clearing she remembers from earlier walks alone. It
is grassy and flat, open on one side to the narrow valley,
enclosed on three sides by cliffs and trees. The wind
plays over our bodies, pine-smelling with a hint of an
edge to it. She tells me how she would walk these trails
alone when I was gone, talking with me in her head.
In her fantasies we never disagreed. Sometimes now we
do and it always surprises her.

I lie back, shading my eyes from the sun, inhale
peace. She stretches out beside me, cutting off the bright-
ness, tickling my lips with grass. I study her lovely fea-
tures, the steady brow and even gaze, the cornsilk-
colored hair. Fragments of song drift through my mind:
"Loving you . . . Loving."

A hawk drifts by and we watch until it disappears
behind a fold in the land. She helps me to my feet and,
holding my hand, leads me to a series of small pools
and waterfalls she has found. I smile my appreciation,
wanting her to know how special this sharing of her
private places is to me.

We return to her cabin by a different trail, passing
budding horsetails, seedling teasel, wild ginger. We walk
slowly, arms entwined, breasts pressing against forearms.
Arriving at the cabin we find our passion reawakened
with no time to assuage it. We kiss and part with diffi-
culty, kiss again, then gather up our afternoon supplies
and hurry down the hill to work.

I am acutely aware of her across the room, glancing
up at times to hold my eyes, blow me a kiss. I admire

her concentration, enjoy working with her, respect her decisions.

At five the others leave and we draw together as if under some aegis, some compulsion to unite. "I want you," I tell her. "I want you now." We scramble up the ladder to the carpeted loft and fall wildly upon each other against the corner pillows.

My arms and legs ache with longing for her, my pelvis throbs. We roll together, legs pressed to pubic bones, hands clutching buttocks, shoulders, tongues caressing lips and necks. I squeeze my thighs against her answering pressure, she rocks against me with little humping motions. Riding dykes they used to call women who could come this way. Riding.

My pants are soaked, my breath is ragged. I hang on to her like the stallion I used to ride, hang on to her while my spirit soars and my pubes clench and unclench, reaching for fullness. My arching back pushes us both off the floor and I can tell she's coming too, riding her own dream and my taut muscles into a land where we are alone together. I peak and cascade in a riot of spasms. Her coming swings us from side to side.

It's dark outside. We hear people enter and move around below us, wait for them to leave, not wanting to share our intimacy. When they depart, we retrace our steps by feel and memory, climb the hill together hand in hand.

While preparing supper she tells me about being short on funds before I arrived so she hitchhiked into town to save on gas. She returned with backpack full: ten pounds of cheese, ten pounds of potatoes, onions, apples, carrots. She wanted to have enough to last the month. Tonight, we're eating bulgur, comfrey, cheddar. Her parents tease her about living on porridge and beans in this vegetarian community.

We eat supper sitting up in bed because there is only one chair and we want to stay close together. I finish

37

my food first and, still turned on from our earlier lovemaking, decide to masturbate.

I set my bowl on the shelf behind me and spread the folds of my kimono from the belt down, She watches me, still eating. I wet my fingers in my mouth and moisten the valley between outer and inner lips, pressing my hair to the sides.

"You're not really going to, are you?" she asks. "You'll ruin my supper."

"Ruin?"

"You know what I mean," plaintively. "How can I eat if you're going to do *that*?"

The imp in me responds by lubricating my fingers again, stroking myself, humming. She sets her dish on the shelf and crawls down on the bed, putting her face close to watch. I wonder if I can come with someone looking on, note the concentration on her face, almost wonder.

She moves the candle to the window ledge, near her head, leaving my face in shadow. I close my eyes and search out an old fantasy about a lover wanting me to masturbate for her entertainment. The fantasy is safer somehow than the real lover watching and I go with it, imagining myself doing what in truth I am doing, knowing that tonight's reality will become a fantasy for future use.

When I come, she is so appreciative, so grateful for my sharing my self-loving with her that I wish I'd thought to do it sooner, am warmed by her response. Settling in beside me, she hugs me, reassures me, tells me about having wanted other lovers to touch themselves in her presence. I rest against her, all limp and happy. She picks up her journal and starts to make notations.

"Are you writing about what just happened?" I ask.

"Yes," she answers, smiling, warm.

"Will you read it to me sometime?"

"If you'd like."

"Yes," I tell her. "I always like the way you write, want to see what happened through your eyes."

☆ ☆ ☆

We have taken the day off, so I am outside in the sunshine, washing my hair in a basin, having heated two pots of water after breakfast. Christine is chopping wood, smiles at me as she carries armloads inside. I settle on the hillside to comb my hair dry, cherishing the rare sun and warmth during this damp and chilly spring. Purple shooting stars blossom at my feet.

Later, we gather kindling twigs into boxes, insurance against the rains that will surely come again. I feel so comfortably at peace with her, wonder if my life could always be like this.

After lunch we look through her picture albums. I'm trying to visually sort out her family, friends and former loves, remember the names of her dogs. How caringly she has photographed her lovers; their faces glow with openness and trust. There is an orderliness about her picture albums that I find compelling, so different from my piles and filing boxes. Her correspondence and her journals are catalogued as well.

She is surprised when I tell her that her landscape photographs are beautiful, something which seems so obvious to me. Her pleasure in my term "nature study" delights me and I run my fingers over the soft light hairs on her cheek. She takes my hand in her mouth and starts to suck on my fingers. I feel my nipples go hard and begin to tingle, then I feel it farther down. She caresses my palm with her tongue, watching for my response from the corners of her eyes, smiling slightly. I grin at her, encourage the seduction.

Carefully, she folds the book and puts it aside, then pulls me down with her so we can stretch out on the narrow bed. "I'm crazy about you," I tell her. "Mummmmm," she says and covers my face with little soft kisses. I feel so warm and melting inside, loving

39

her and feeling loved by her, desire and delight playing across her face.

"Let's undress and get under the covers," she says. We do and once again I marvel at the delicate beauty of her bones, the sloping grandeur of her breasts. I bury my face in her, sniffing at the warm and different odors rising from our bodies, incense, musk. She strokes me with long fluid movements and I relax into her hands. Below, I'm dewy wet and open to her gently probing fingers.

"Go inside," I tell her. "Go inside, I want you there."

She does and I moan and wrap my arms around her neck, one foot behind her knee, press my lips against her skin below the collar bone. I want her to understand so much that I still don't have the words to say. How I have opened my spirit to her.

Her fingers dart and thrust, rapid, playful. I laugh because I never used to come this way, and now I know I will soon, again, can feel the heavy warm sensations spread. My muscles clamp around her, thrust my pelvis up. I grab her arm, hold her still, deep inside me, sense the spasm throb and squeeze, orgasm brimming.

Relaxing, I think about the happy faces of her lovers, feel a kinship with them. Sighing, I know I want to come again soon so ask her to touch me outside and drift up to meet her slippery fingers, tracing delicate patterns around my clitoris. Dreamy, I seem to be floating over forests, mists, and streams. Slowly, I sense my climax building, drawing me to her, gathering my energies, my whole awareness into one fine, glowing point that is a seed, my clitoris. She touches me steady, my response rocks my limbs and sends the covers flying. She pulls them back up over us, settles me into the haven of her arms and kisses my heavy eyelids, murmuring endearments.

I ask her about sex with other people, was it always easy? How has it grown? She tells me about introducing oral sex into an ongoing relationship. She had known

40

about it intellectually for quite awhile, but had waited until the impulse to do it had motivated her. I like the ways she combines intelligence, knowledge, and feelings. Feel I can bring more of myself alive with her than I have been able to do with others.

Wanting to say thank you for the pleasure she has given me, I slide beneath the covers, part her fur, and nestle in. Worshipping her with my lips and tongue, I go soft all over, touch her with loving hands. Her crest rises to me, her lips fill and spread. Gently, I coax her to me, finger inside her nave, mouth warm and tender: prolonged rhythmic repetition. She comes to me with splashes of sound, unexpected.

"Yes. Yes. Yes."

I curl up between her legs, finger inside her still, kiss her lightly, press my cheek against her wet and fragrant hair.

Rousing, lethargic, I stroke back her hair again, try to impress the look of her upon my memory. Her labia are shell pink, wild rose pink, small and delicate, fluted at the edges. She has a tiny freckle on one inner lip, others scattered between and on the outer lips, friendly-seeming. I marvel at the minute ruffles, passion's lace. They remind me of the cochina shells I gathered as a child, savoring their beauty and their broth.

I tell her about a story by Anais Nin that described a woman putting lipstick on her nether lips, her 'sex' as Nin called them, while admirers and would-be suitors watched. I find the description of that semi-public activity to be exciting still. Christine has started caressing me as I talk. Quite suddenly, I feel myself go all soft and moist with desire. Christine notices the changes in my body, my breathing, begins to rub her face across my breasts, licking and pulling on each nipple as she passes it. Squeezing my nipples with her hands, she slowly begins to move down my body, trailing her hair along my skin.

41

Stretched between my legs, she seeks me with her tongue, presses me, damp to damp. She slides her hands down to cup my ass and I caress my own breasts, sink into the luxury of her loving. Her tongue, her lips, her hands are spreading warmth all over me. I breathe and rock, I croon to her, I rub my feet along her back. I feel so cared for, so appreciated. She keeps shifting patterns, playing with my response. I chase after her, rippling to her touch. My loins are throbbing, rolling in her hands, longing now for more sensation, more pressure, more speed.

She becomes the follower giving all I've asked for, eating me with a hard, steady consistency. Remembering the Nin story, I imagine my sex bright red and swollen, neon, iridescent. I spread out from that glowing center in pulsating waves of light, crying out, coming, holding her head and crying; pulling her up to cover me, hold me, reassure me. I feel so fragile, so open. Warming me, murmuring to me, she makes my world safe again.

☆ ☆ ☆

We spend the night in a hotel, refurbished relic of a more elegant era. I cut Christine's hair, taking care to avoid the cowlicks, then we climb into the bathtub and shower together. Living in her cabin we have taken only towel baths, using her enameled basin, heating water on the small wood stove. Now, we luxuriate in the unlimited hot water, soaping each other repeatedly, caressing through the bubbles.

I shampoo her hair, knead the scalp with all my fingers, spread foam to the amber brush under her arms, the curly bush where her legs come together. Rinsing the bubbles free, I kneel in the spray and lick her clitoris, gently finger the sides of her cervix, that playful little friend. She begins to shake, then collapses around me, promising more later.

Since she has known for a long time that I enjoy water stimulation, I suggest she join me as I masturbate. She agrees with obvious delight.

42

I have her sit at the back of the tub with legs stretched forward. Patiently, I test and retest the water until satisfied with the temperature and delicate flow. I sit, facing away from her, toward the faucet, then lie back and slide my bottom under the water, knees bent, feet against the wall tiles. I ask her to move forward until my head rests in her lap, her thighs support my shoulder.

I rub her breasts with fondness, then close my eyes and go down into my body until I reach that so soft liquid touching I first found when I was seven. I use one hand to cut off the flow periodically, tease myself, rest awhile then release the fall and let my tension build again. My leg muscles twitch and jump. I caress one breast, both breasts, relax, tense again.

I dream the water is licking me, loving me, fondling my stomach and my ass. I sense Christine's nearness; appreciate her unobtrusive presence, hands gently resting on my shoulders. I breathe in the warm mist and begin to stroke my shaft, pulling back the covering from my bud. My hand begins to move faster, almost of its own volition. I remind myself that my body knows what she wants, how to move without my conscious thought. Relax, focus, breathe faster, let my inner self lead.

I squeeze one nipple, feel the tendons in my neck grow tighter, pulling my head back, my jaw down. Please let her not think me ugly. Let this be a joy we can share. The water licks my softness, laps around my torso, touches me with delicate, sharp spray fingers.

I expand into sensations, reach for that intense point just short of satiation, hold it, hold myself open as my body buckles, closing in around myself, raising me away from Christine's legs up toward my knees and then releasing me slowly, like an ocean's wash from side to side.

I roll into a fetal position, curling between her legs. She murmurs loving words to me: how pretty I am, how much she cares.

We climb out of the enclosure and towel each other dry. The bedroom seems toasty with the heat turned high.

I stretch out on the bed and she rubs my back, sensuously and slowly like she did that first time. When I turn over, she positions her vulva above my face and begins to lick my labia, darting her tongue into my vagina, causing internal sparks to shoot around my body, along my limbs. I separate her folds and press my lips against her cleft, move my head from side to side. I search out the faint smell of her, draw down the soft liquid, say a prayer of thanks for this blessing, this sacrament.

She must have a finger inside me from the way I feel all full inside, feel that more generalized pleasure that penetration brings added to the exquisite blaze pulsing from my clitoris. What I am doing to her merges with what she is doing to me, blends with our humming sounds, the feeling of enclosed, protected space. I feel weightless, surrounded by warm loving, peak and relax with a sustained sense of excitement.

I start to buck and come first, holding onto her bottom and resting my lips against her, then licking, touching, we roll to the side. I continue tonguing her until she comes like the blasting out of small explosions, barely contained inside her skin. My arms pull her thighs against my face, blurring her sounds.

She curves her body around mine. "Did you deliberately hold off coming, trying to climax at the same time I did?" she asks.

"No, I wouldn't do that to my body. When an orgasm rises, I just let it come."

Christine seems pleased by my answer, holds me for a while, then opens her journal.

April

I have lived with Christine in her cabin for a month. She is driving me now to catch my plane home. I feel tingly, expectant, excited.

"Would you like it if I came to live near you?" The words burst out of my mouth, almost of their own volition.

"Yes. Oh, yes." She looks terribly young and filled with pleasure.

We are both quiet for a while. We notice daffodils blooming in the grass median. At the airport cafe, I pick up a book of matches which bears the motto "Eat Out More Often." We are cheered by it, share a conspiratorial grin.

A screwdriver in her coat pocket sets off the security alarm and I wait for her to turn it in, hurry to join me. We are wearing our public faces, kiss discreetly and part.

I return home to find that a budget cut has eliminated my summer job. The building I have lived in for eight years has been sold. New owners want my apartment. Fate seems to be giving me a shove.

I call Leah, an old lover with whom I am still good friends. She listens to my news, my options, and my fears.

"You just love order," she says, "knowing where things are and what's happening. So maybe this won't last forever. What does? Why don't you just enjoy it? Go along for the ride?"

I call my aunt, recount recent events. She gives sympathy and support. I tell her I'm considering packing everything and moving north. She answers that she's always liked my descriptions of Christine, desires my happiness. She reminds me of my childhood love of mountains.

I stew, resentful over the move, timid in the face of emotional commitment.

Sleeping, I dream I'm skiing, skating, riding bumper cars in an amusement park. I wake and pace, return to bed to sleep and dream of swimming, dream myself a dolphin swimming in green water. Another dolphin comes to swim beside me, disappears then reappears, nudges me playfully, then swims away. I feel calm, drop beyond any memory of dreams, sleep, and wake with image of the dolphin and the water, vivid in my mind.

I phone a message to Christine, asking her to call me back. When she does, I tell her I'm moving north. Her pleasure makes all this worthwhile.

I locate a mover, send out emergency letters, finish what I can, apologize for commitments I can't fulfill.

I begin having pains in my abdomen near my right ovary. I pray they will go away, will not turn out to be appendicitis.

I'm relieved when everything's finally packed, mailed, and/or sold. I schedule farewell dinners with friends — nostalgia, warmth, good wine.

"Well, that's that," my great-aunt Grace says inside my head. "Life goes on." And indeed it does.

Christine is waiting for me when I arrive, smiling and crying at the same time.

May

Searching for a place to live, we stay overnight in
a cheap motel with a vibrating bed. She can't believe I'd
spend money on this nonsense but joins me on the jig-
gling bed and agrees it's pleasurable. We shower, then
return to the bed where she stands before me and teasingly begins to touch herself. I am instantly attentive,
want to hold her, want to watch. Inspired by her glowing there before me, I ask her if she'll hold the position,
let me draw the image of her hand and cunt. She agrees.
I locate my pad and pencils with shaking fingers, quiver
in my rush to catch the moment, claim her body for
my own.

She's amazed by the process, how concentrated I
am, how quickly done.

The drawing radiates power, focuses on her strong
hands, wiry hair, soft flesh. I prop it near the mirror and
push her down against the bed, bury my face in her
tender, excited crotch. Kneeling, I lick and suck her clitoris, lick a finger and slide it into her bottom. Her hips
push up, commanding my attentions. Lady, you are dynamite, I think to her. She wiggles more, makes tiny
yelping sounds, comes hard, squeezing down everywhere.

"Hummmmmmm . . . I love you," I trail in wet little
kisses across her tummy. She sniffs me, holds and licks
my face, looks deeply and with pleasure into my eyes.

"Lady, you're dynamite," I tell her.

"Yeah," she says, "you too."

☆ ☆ ☆ ☆

We find and move into a new home, everything sitting around in boxes, waiting. I set up the stereo first so we can have music to work by, put on "Favorite Waltzes" by the Mom and Pops. Christine is busy so I slip into a "little bit of nothing" black dress from the Salvation Army, add long, fake pearls and return to see if I can distract her.

I slide my hand along her bottom where she's leaning over, buried in a deep box. Once I have her attention I turn up the music and start twirling the beads, vamping for her entertainment. Half closing her eyes, she takes me in her arms and starts to move, managing somehow to look down at me even though we're the same height. I have a special fondness for the "Tennessee Waltz" and every time it comes around, I smile at her for the full three minutes.

After awhile we stop dancing and just sway in time with the music, kissing and stroking each other's bodies. She gathers a couple of pillows and we stretch out on the carpet, still nuzzling and necking. She slides her hand under my dress, up my thigh to where my panties would be if I had any on. She's being cool tonight so pretends she's not surprised even though she probably is. I adore her when she's being all sultry and bar-dykey and keep giving her my best southern belle come hither looks. She is pressing her index finger lengthwise along my pubertal crevice and I know I may lose my composure at any minute so enjoy our drama while it lasts.

I lose it, close my eyes and turn my head against my rising shoulder as I spread my legs to let her in. Inside me, she slowly moves her fingers in big circles, watching my passion rise, making me want her. I am draped around her, one leg caught between hers, the other foot braced against her thigh, pushing down, bottom lifting to thrust against her circles.

"Please, Christine, please—more, more." I feel her chuckle, start an in-and-out motion, rapid, one, two, three,

48

pause, repeat. This woman drives me wild sometimes, my body a hot fiery river flowing under her hands. The "Tennessee Waltz" is on again as I lose myself to her fingers, to the music. I am rolling, pulling her with me, crying out with an aching so intense I almost want her to stop. Almost.

And like all orgasms, it does subside, this one slowly ebbing away into the dreamy night and another song.

I spread myself on top along her length, begin to undulate against her, pubic bone to pubic bone. Tribadism they say it's called, this moving each against the other's body. Tribad: a woman who loves women. My, how I do love this woman. She's the one with eyes closed this time, mouth slightly open, chin up.

I work my way down along her rib cage, unbuttoning as I go. I pull her jeans and pants all the way off and stretch out before her pussy, fondling her gently, pushing back the frothing hairs. I love you, I say with my body, tongue along the hollow separating outer from inner lips. "I love you," I whisper and dart my tongue into the liquid pooling in her vulval hollow. "Love you," licking and pressing down, swinging my head from side to side.

Bracing on one arm, I reach up and rub my thumb across her swollen shaft with gratifying results. She's very noisy tonight. Her coming has the intensity of an explosion followed by repeated aftershocks. I hang on tightly so she won't bang her delicate parts hard against my teeth. Afterward, she is so quiet I think she must have fallen asleep but no, she opens her eyes just a little and smiles wanly at me then burrows against my shoulder and relaxes again. The Mom and Pops waltz on.

☆ ☆ ☆

She brings me a fawn lily, says it reminds her of my breast, maculated, spotted. She returns to her work while I go into the kitchen, looking for a vase. As I put the flower in water, I imagine that she kneels behind me, raises my kaftan and starts to knead my labial folds.

49

I laugh at her, try to pull away. She grips me tighter, begins to lick me from behind. I lean over the sink, swaying, find it hard to breath. In my fantasy, she pushes at me with tongue and fingers, finds me pliant. I put my head down, close my eyes, spread for her. I imagine she's a stranger, interrupting the flow of my day with carnal demands. I sink further into her soft, moist insistence, into my dream.

With a sculling motion, she moulds my front, assaults my rear. Resistance would be counterproductive. I want her to claim me, enter me with overwhelming hunger, take me in her time, by her will. Thumb and fingers inside me, she increases the bond between us, summons forth a rush of feeling. I mutiny briefly, defy her, dissolve in a wash of sensation, free both of us in the discharge of my passion.

I notice I'm still holding the flower, put it in the vase, go looking for Christine. Finding her, I tell her of my fantasy, watch her get excited.

She hurries me into the house, her eyes all merry and bright, her voice husky. We make love on the rug, the bed, tangle in the covers, laugh, come. I remember reading that oral sex helps uncover and focus the third eye, think about how powerfully our loving has caused my work to flower. I run my fingers over the spots on my breast, think of the lily, dream.

Breasts, I'm rolling my face against her breasts. She's pulling on mine, pinching and tweaking the nipples, squeezing the mass in her so-soft hands. Shifting, kneeling over me, she sucks and kneads them, pressing in, rolling around. My clit reacts as if it were the center of attention, connected to my bosom by an unbroken, tingling, sputtering wire. I flash and sweat, burying my fingers in her hair. My hips heave and she presses harder, encircling, oscillating. Writhing, twitching, I foam and shiver, convulse and quake. Gasping, I beg her to stop, pull on her hair.

"Did you really come?" she asks.

"I think so," I answer. "It sure felt as if I did. Kinsey says that some of us come from breast stimulation alone, but I never have before."

She chuckles, shakes her head and chuckles again. I cool my face against her skin, feel my breathing slow, taut muscles go slack. I'm loving her so fully, amazed at how I travel with her, how I lift beyond my momentary flesh.

Calming, I work my way along her torso, nibbling, nudging. Finding her hair moist, I bury my lips against hers, lap at holy waters, bathe in sacred springs.

> She is present, banquet, mother, earth
> I am hungry
> She is Hunger
> I am wanting
>   acting
> She is yearning
>   brimming
>   spilling
> She is calling loudly
>   lightly
> She is coming
>   in my hands
>   under my tongue.

Loving. Let me spread my loving over you, I think and spread my body over hers, wiping my face as I move, smiling.

I get up, put a record on, begin to dance for her. She leans back, watching, intent, attentive. I approach, retreat, suggestive, lewd. I approach again, snake my body along her, poke my tongue into her belly button, nibble at her core. I hover between her legs, dance my hands along her body. Settling, I raise her hips: chalice, nectar, guava, honey. Sacred honey. Christine, honey, love you. Love you. I am fluid with the music, liquid, darting, gathering her sweet and salty quim.

51

☆ ☆ ☆

It's late spring and we are helping friends by pick-axing a drainage ditch behind one of their buildings. Since I have never used a pickax before, I spend some time locating its balance, my center. We alternate axing and hauling away the water-soaked muck. The soil is red clay, somewhat rubbery, sticks to our skin and clothes in bright splashes.

We touch each other intimately as we pass in the narrow gully between bank and building. During one break we start to neck. Christine goes to pee into the can on the porch, returns, gloves in pockets, fastening her pants. Lasciviously, I rub my heavily clothed labia against her bent and braced thigh, caress taut nipples, pushing through her shirt. Shifting she opens my pants, slides her hand inside and down, spreading my legs wider. My boots slip in the mud. She tightens her grip around my waist until I regain my balance. I prop one boot against the wall and press against her, hungry.

She slips inside me, starts to fuck me quick and hard, her knuckles rubbing firmly on my glans. I wiggle my torso back and forth, up and down, more, more. She whispers encouragement, "Yes, yes, love, let it come." I feel like I'm pulling everything into my pelvis: her fingers, my labia, and asshole. I hold my breath for as long as I can, gulp air, and hold my breath again; think I can't maintain this tension much longer. All of my being is wound into one tight ball, somewhere in my middle.

With that wonderfully intuitive awareness she has about me, she knows where to touch and how to move, knows I'm going to peak soon, gazes at me soft and open, rubs my clitoris with her thumb. I close my eyes again and wait in that quiet, hollow feeling place until I see the flames licking out behind closed lids, feel my shoulders hunch and then convulse. Shuddering, I come and come.

Slowly, I return, cling to her, breathing in heavy short gasps. The odors of sweat and love mingle with smells of damp wood and sun-warmed grass. I kiss and lick her salty neck, push her gently against the building, work my boots more firmly into the clay. We kiss for a long time before I go in search of her wetness. She sighs as I enter her, rest there for a while, then bring the moisture out and up around her pearl. Moaning, she turns her head from side to side, draws me on with the darting pelvic thrusts which I find so exciting. I flatten my fingers, move them between her inner lips, rub my face and lips against her cheek.

Her knees begin to wobble. I grasp her leg with mine, push her more firmly against the building with my weight. She presses her mons hard against my fingers till I reach inside with short, deep thrusts. "Oh, how wet she is," I sing inside. I tell her she is very wet. She rocks upon my fingers, then brings my hand out again. I return to her hooded lady, rub the head and shaft with slippery silken fingers, separate the hairs.

Her head is thrown back, neck arched forward, shoulders shaking. Little quakes run up and down her body, she starts to vibrate all over. I am full of loving her, wanting her joy. She quivers, then seems to shatter around my cupped and writhing fingers, vagina opening to me, clenching around my knuckles in thigh-squeezing bursts.

At home that evening, we talk about our afternoon loving, linger over favorite moments, warm and close. Turned on again, I tense my heavy limbs and clasp her leg between my own. We rub and talk and tease until we both come again, fingers and toes curled tight. We laugh and hug, amazed at this river of passion that runs beneath us, rising to our surface and taking us, sometimes abruptly, giving little warning of the depth and power that will surge and crest, subside and leave us shaken and spent.

June

The dry, sparkling days of summer have arrived. Grass turns brown, then gold and white. Wild cherries ripen, raspberries flesh out, blackberries glisten. In damp areas the teasel blooms. Honeysuckle drapes tiny white and violet blossoms over limbs. On dry slopes lupine bunches: white and yellow, purple and blue.

Christine goes off daily to work on a magazine, returns drained. I volunteer to make dinner for the three weeks that this will continue. I'm building a darkroom where a washer and dryer once stood, settling in, preparing artwork for some long-time clients.

When I go for a medical checkup, my pap smear shows a class three dysplasia once again. I feel sick with worry but decide, on the advice of a general practitioner, to visit a naturopath. I want to try some alternative forms of healing before allowing the more radical treatments to be used on my body. Although I know I don't want children, I want to avoid the trauma of surgery, if possible.

Complicating my distress, one of Christine's old loves wants to visit her at this time. Thankfully, Christine puts her off. My psyche is on overload.

July

One afternoon we pick blackberries. At twilight, berry pie baking, a thunderstorm passes, announcing an early autumn. We make love comfortingly, familiarly, hands and lips reaching, darting. We roll and cuddle, laugh and come, inebriated with velvety textures, intimate smells.

Expanding the energy, I bring her tea in bed, touch and tease her, lie outside the covers and hug her to me, humping gently. Our play turns serious, intense. Engorged with desire, we push the covers away, grasp and cling. I twine my legs through hers, rub harder, longing to become the universe, break open somehow, become another me.

Clasping, holding, grabbing, binding, caressing her ass, breathing harder, holding breath. I love you, my nipples say to her breast, my nipples hard, erect, inflamed. I love you, my belly says to hers, slippery with sweat, sparkling with sensations.

"I love you," I say, arching and coming and tightening against her, everywhere.

Separating, I press again into her body, thankful for her openness, treasuring the visceral level, tissue-deep response that tells me, repeatedly, that in coming to her I have found a home.

☆ ☆ ☆

We receive a flyer announcing a dance taking place in the barn on locally-owned women's land. I wear a floor length skirt and brightly patterned blouse. She dresses in a backless, red, spaghetti-strapped slinky gown I found for her in a thrift store. She looks gorgeous, fits my fantasies of Leo elegantly partying with straights in Mary Renault's THE MIDDLE MIST. We agree to only dance with each other for the evening since in truth we are going out to be together.

Seductively, she twists and sways before me. I touch her with my eyes. She turns away, beckons me over her shoulder. I circle her, swaying with the music. Through half-closed lids, suggestive movements, she extends to me her come-on. Vibrantly attracted, I spin off, scattering some of my excitement. She insinuates her torso behind me, mirroring my undulations. Lightly she holds my hips, stomach rubbing my ass. I feel moisture running down my legs, lean back and press against her breasts. Raising my arms, I shimmy against her. Delighted, she slides her hands along my rib cage, turns me round and pulls me close.

We slow dance to a couple of fast songs, murmuring love and sexual details. I choose this time to tell her I'm not wearing underpants, am tensing and relaxing my sex muscles, imagining her fingers burrowing there. Her face lights up, eyes twinkle, breasts expand. We separate into jitterbug steps and turns—then disco back, holding each other with our eyes. I press my body firmly to hers, noticing our nipples hard against their fabrics.

I squeeze my ass muscles in time with the bass line, think I've reached an altered state of awareness. The lights around us pulse and swirl. Other dancers blur into a mist of delicate swaying colors. Her face glows faintly from the inside.

Hips touching, we bump and grind, shoulders coiling, hands and lips grazing each other's flesh.

"I want to love you," she says. "I want to love you, there, between your legs, kiss and lick you till you come and come, all ravaged, almost want to beg me to stop

56

but choose to continue until overwhelmed with exhaustion."

"Yes," I answer. "Yes."

When we stop for refreshments, our friends tell us how much they enjoy watching us dance. The voyeur in me wishes I could watch too.

August

After months of visiting naturopaths who have me taking an assortment of vitamins and trace minerals, my pap smear is again a class one. Relief makes me giddy.

We have a three-day vacation, decide to explore local rivers instead of traveling to the coast, which is probably foggy and cold.

I lie back in the hot sand letting it draw the soreness out of my muscles. I listen to the bird calls, dream about her hands soothing me all over.

She races with our newly-acquired puppy, splashing in the shallow water. Periodically, one or both of them stop by my patch of sybaritic indulgence, shake or drip cold water on my sun-warmed skin.

Another day, we follow a back road to where she's heard there is a swimming hole. The small river is exquisite, water low late in the dry season, banks and sandbars lush with growth. Huge, still pools mirror granite boulders. Small side streams jump from basin to pool with glittering abandon.

We gather berries to sweeten our box lunches. The puppy runs enthusiastic circles around us.

> You lick me
> rush inside of me.
> You are the stream
>   the leaves
>   the stillness.
> I am the bed for your river.

☆ ☆ ☆

We're dancing again, this time to live rock 'n roll. The scene is a lush bar turned private club for the evening. I'm feeling glittery, very excited. The room is filled with flashy women.

Christine and I join with friends: a poet/calligrapher/bookbinder, a professor of thoughts and dreams, an astrologer/artist, a window washer.

The food is spread on an upper level: deviled eggs, stuffed mushrooms, raw veggies, chips, creams, and dips. Christine and I share a plate, munch, talk, feed each other. She is wearing green, her long arms lit from within.

We dance slowly, pushing against each other, then faster, sinuous, twisting, angular.

Days later, I leave for a brief business trip, masturbate, manually, lying on my back, remembering the elegance of her moving form. I dream of her dancing, poolside, in the moonlight; dancing on the water, rippling the silver surface to a beat known only to herself. I call to her and she drifts toward me, wraps around me like a stole, begins caressing me through my party gown.

Abruptly, we're swimming in the nighttime ocean, nude, body-surfing in high waves, tumbling and laughing and clinging to each other.

Settling into the wet edges of the sand, she begins tonguing my private lips.

I awaken slowly, hand between my legs, fingers active, pajama bottoms wet. Her presence lingers with me through breakfast and into the unknown city.

September

Late in September we visit her parents, camping out along the way. One cold night, we pull into a campground late, turned on. We kiss in icy, moonlit silence, press against each other, fumble under clothes. I reach inside her jeans, her thermal underwear, her pants, push her against the door.

Having started her period, she is wearing a pad. I move beneath it, find her softness, play her pleasure with my fingers. The cold finally forces us to stop, seek warmth in the restrooms. She makes faces at my brown-encrusted fingers flowing red under the water, blessed.

In the morning we laugh about the passion, the blood. Such a sexy memory for a night when neither of us came.

Her parents are distant at first, guarded, then warm to me, joke, tease in their literate, restrained, ironic way. Her father, a writer, entertains me with pirate stories, family histories. Her mother feeds me until I fear I'll pop. Nights, we snuggle but find sex impossible in their home.

As we head back to our own nest, the urgency of our desire swells, I lean against her as she drives, touch her nipples, slip my hand between her legs. I tell her how beautiful she is, how desirable, how I want to lick and suck and fuck her, how I want to put my fingers and tongue inside her, kiss her lips and ears and ass.

Opening the house up, I open to her too. We make love in the living room, on the couch, hard, demanding, still partially dressed. I come and come, want more and come again. Her pleasure is harsh, hungry. I feed it, deep. When we wake, we're still entangled, eat standing in the kitchen and go to bed.

November

I awaken at 6:30 to find her sparkling at me.

"Do you want your presents now? Can I bring you coffee?"

"Oh, yes."

All week the beautifully wrapped presents sat enticingly in the living room — "I love you," spelled out in bright ribbon, one word to each package.

Christine brings the coffee, packages, and envelopes and spreads them around me on the bed. In one is a book I've longed for. In another is a C-clamp, a friendly helping hand. Finally, there is a digital clock radio. I read all the instructions, want to plug it in, see if I can set the time right.

She brings me breakfast in bed, later makes love to me with her hands, cradling me, crooning to me. My orgasm, a giant purple wave, rolls across my body, oceanic.

Guests arrive from all over. Two drive eight hours to get here, singing all the way. Others fly in, arriving with stories of hitching from the country airport because the limo driver wanted to wait an hour for the next flight.

I've invited a variety of people. Many have never met before. The invitation suggested that they dress in Salvation Army Gaudy.

I dress slinky. Christine puts on her "Amazon Dolly Parton" persona complete with lush, blonde wig. No one recognizes her.

People keep piling out of cars, setting up tents in the back yard, arriving at the house marvelously, outrageously attired. I melt into a luxury of smells and sounds. Colors glow and flash and mingle. Christine has brought me roses. The cake is covered with roses so that everyone can have one. I drift from group to group, hugging, touching, happy.

In the bathroom, I wonder who has been changing the toilet paper; in the kitchen I notice the order, feel gifted by my friends. I meet Christine's eyes briefly across the room and everything around me gently, softly fades. When it's time for the cake, I blow out all forty candles, pleased by the murmurs of pleasure around me.

☆ ☆ ☆

I am waiting for Christine in the 3 a.m. chill of a strange city. She is arriving by bus after an all-night ride. I've been traveling on business for two weeks. Three buses pull in before hers.

Anxiously, I watch for her face, relax deeply when she steps off the bus, sees me, smiles. We sit in the car, kissing, touching, affirming, until the cold becomes unbearable.

Safely settled in the soft double bed at a friend's house, we make love with the hunger of our separation, fall asleep as the sky lightens, wake to good food, exciting conversations.

The next day we go to a Thanksgiving retreat located in a campsite ringed by rugged mountains. The workshops are diverse and exciting. Although we know some of the women present, many faces are new and the stories that go with them are all interesting.

By the afternoon of the second day, Christine wants to connect with me again by making love. We are sleeping in a cabin with six other women. I am tense, not wanting someone to walk in on us. In response to Christine's hunger and my need for privacy, I hang bathrobes and one of the sleeping bags from the upper bunk, creating a small burrow for us.

Reluctant still, I lie back in her arms, pressing my lips against hers. Her mouth is so soft, so expressive, tongue grasshoppering along, among, between my lips. She pushes my legs apart with one of her own and begins an oscillating motion, kissing me still and rotating one of my breasts in the palm of her hand. My sensations create a commotion pushing my fears into the background.

We thrust against each other's thighs; the momentum, once established, seems to continue almost of its own volition. We move like trees on a breezy day. My body is a dancer in the treetops, feathered by the leaves. Her body, supple branches, twines around mine, respondent, receptive. She works her hand between us, fingers my clit. I reach out to her in spirit, cleave to her with my torso, growl and purr a song of love.

I come first then slide into oblivion, surface worrying that someone may have heard us. We neck for a few minutes before I duck my head outside our curtains, thankful to find we're still alone. Returning to her body I snuggle in, my fingers answering her need. She's wet and slippery, voracious, accepting. I fuck her deep inside, rolling two fingers around her cervix, concentrating on that forward spot that elicits remarkable response.

I move to kneel between her legs, fingers still inside her, lick her swollen, hardening crest. She murmurs encouragement, rises to meet me, combs her fingers through my hair. Holding her clitoris between my lips, lightly I rock my head from side to side, bring my thumb forward to caress the softness just below the glans. Her pleasure is so immensely gratifying, my body vibrates in a rhythm matching her own.

I think I hear someone enter the cabin, decide to continue, hope they won't be offended, won't be straight, won't be aggressively celibate, won't be nosy.

Christine has crested several times already, now her muscles clamp down in primal demand, pulsate in systemic pleasure and subside into aftershocks. I meander up her body to her shoulder, carefully keeping my fingers inside her.

"Ouuuuu," she whispers. "That was soooo nice." I agree, am thankful that her will prevailed. When we emerge later, whoever I had heard has gone. In the evening, one of the women gently teases us about taking "private pleasures."

December

For the holidays, I make Christine a doll with velour skin, sparkling eyes, and long pigtails just like Christine wore as a child. I give her pink velvet labia and a soft vaginal pouch. I make little blue jeans for her and a tank top and find a baby's sweater at a thrift shop that just fits. Christine reads aloud to me as I sew, stories by Lewis Carroll, a biography of Louisa May Alcott. I call the doll "Little Christine" and the human Christine, who wasn't interested in dolls at all as a child, goes all soft as I put the doll in her arms.

I make a doll for myself, too, using an elf pattern, all skinny-long arms and legs and big eyes. I call her Elf and dress her in a long embroidered robe.

Sometimes while I work, I remember evenings in my childhood when my grandmother would sit turning my grandad's collars or crocheting intricate lace table-cloths that looked like spider's webs. My grandad sat near her repairing his fishing nets — bigger spider webs. I would crochet chains or draw or improvise doll clothes. I wasn't allowed to use a needle yet, although I did thread Grandmother's at night when she said her eyesight wasn't good. What would she think, I wonder, of the rosy little vulva I give my doll? Of the erect nipples and tidy anus?

I just don't know.

Christine's doll and mine spend some time getting to know each other. Elf is much more aggressive than I was as a child and wants to play "doctor" immediately.

Little Christine suggests they build a fort in the Christmas tree instead. So they spend their first few days together in the lower limbs of an elegant fir.

One night I come into the living room to find that Christine has undressed her doll and is examining her with great interest. Later, I find the doll sitting naked in my rocking chair.

"She told me she didn't want to put her clothes back on," Christine informs me.

The doll is still undressed the following day, so I bring Elf from under the tree and tuck her in beside her friend. Not wanting Little Christine to feel isolated in her all-togethers, I remove Elf's garment and cover both dolls with a large cotton scarf. In the days that follow we change their positions, demonstrating an intimate knowledge of each other and the pleasurable activities in which two female bodies can engage.

The electrician, arriving to deal with a kitchen problem, thankfully does not seem to notice what is going on in the rocker. I drop a pillow over the dolls as unobtrusively as I can.

☆ ☆ ☆

The night before Christmas we spend in the kitchen preparing turkey, dressing, sharing stories of other years, both good and bad. Many deaths have occurred in my family just before Christmas, people argued, drank too much, mourned, fought. Christine's orderly nuclear family dined alone together, then joined with a small group of friends for quiet sharing.

Christine reads aloud to me: A CHILD'S CHRISTMAS IN WALES, John Wahtera's THE HAPPENING. Her voice is so rich and expressive, I follow different characters — visualizing the action, cry at the end.

We clean the kitchen then open the living room couch into a bed and lie embracing before the fire, listening to a record of holiday music. The tree winks at us, gives the room a glow of rosy mystery, reminding me of evening services at Notre Dame. Christine eases

67

her weight on top of me, cradles my face, picks out gossamer patterns around my lips, begins to dart inside. I hold her, delicious, receptive.

She begins to undulate, hard against my pubic bone, grazing my breasts. My nipples feel like bells chiming, vibrations rippling through them, their hardness both announcement and invitation.

I settle in for a long ride, feel the lubrication trickle down my ass; sweat breaks out under my arms, along my skin. I flush repeatedly. We rock in unison as if buoyed by some great ocean, immoderate, continuing.

I dream myself dough, compressed by her; clay, informed by her; down she comes against me, down she comes again, again. I stiffen with my own excitement, bend to meet her, strain to merge. Sometimes her downy cheek's against mine, sometimes her mouth, her lips, her tongue demanding. From a long way off I hear my own voice grating, more, begging for more. Wailing, I cry out my love, fired by desire. My need becomes devouring. I clutch her shoulders, breathe in little gasps.

She revolves around my fire, relentless pressure, primal nest. I open in all my silent untouched places, releasing longings that I didn't know I had. Unsealed, I immerse myself in her, wallow in sensations, roll and moan.

My need for release pulls me into focus, requires satisfaction. Here, take care of me, it cries out, insistent. I tense, cling to her, squeeze my legs together, let my body lead: sunrise, Aurora Borealis. Rose-tipped, twisting, I come against her, come unto her, praising love.

She moves against me gently until my strength returns, then, clutching my leg between her own, she brings about her own conclusion, pushing away from me, head back, eyes closed, lips pursed.

I pray briefly to Our Lady of Sorrows for guidance and protection, this loving is so rich, I want it to last.

January

The fire burns hot in the cast-iron stove, flickers through glass doors, across our bodies. She's been reading to me from old journals, letting me know her younger self. Outside, the weather storms across the mountains, cuts us off from other worlds. She lights candles, I start incense burning. We know we're going to make love. The preparations are a form of foreplay. I bring in the oil, put it next to the extended couch, think I want her to go into my bottom. She notes the oil with half-closed lids, the flicker of a smile.

She massages me into indolent, anticipatory excitement, turns me over and begins to concentrate on my abdomen, my ass, my genitalia. Taking more oil, she makes small forays into my anus, moistening the opening, relaxing the ring of muscle. I spread my legs, knees bent, push down slightly to facilitate her entry.

The palm of her other hand pushes steadily against my mons, my clitoris.

She goes deeper into my rear, holds her movements until the muscle unclenches, lets her in further, then further still.

She pauses again, watching my face, attentive to my breathing. I open my secret places to her, allow the withheld sensations to spread.

I wiggle encouragingly against her finger, buried deep. She moves it in slow circles, exploring, testing, then raises my legs over her shoulders and starts to fuck

69

me, relaxed, receptive. I raise my arms, hang on to the back of the sofa.

Today, the whole environment seems eroticized. A low, husky singing fills the room, hazy with incense and flickering candles. I tell her I don't want to come too fast, she rests inside me as I breathe deeply, slowly. I remember another time when she curled behind me, entering both my openings. Her free arm reaching 'round to gently finger my small, sacred mountain. Then, as now, it was cold outside. We had been sleeping on the sofa bed, stretched out in front of another fire.

I stir, undulate against her impaling finger, her caressing thumb. Her presence increases with each breath, each movement. I tense, relax, tense again. My arms and legs quiver, tremble. My belly shakes. I come around her, lights flashing behind my eyes.

☆ ☆ ☆

Christine goes north on a business trip which will include a visit with her parents. My first night alone I sleep with the light on, awaken early, restless. The second morning, I feel clearly turned on, lie on my back touching my labia with both hands, chasing the sensations with childhood abandon. My orgasm is quick, brief, intense. I slip into sleep again and dream of Christine licking me, squeezing my breasts. I carry the dream with me into the day, dedicate the fruit on my cereal to my loving, praise Christine at midday, sit long into the twilight remembering desire.

I awaken every morning to my body, please myself with long caresses, sometimes on my stomach, sometimes on my back. On the evening of the fourth day I masturbate in the bathtub, candles lit, incense smoky. The water reaches into me like fingers, massages my stiffness, dissipates tensions. I float in a timeless place, the water lapping at me, the dim light lulling me. My first and second comings are gentle and filled with pastel colors: rose, mauve. My third is an extended benediction as I cry out in pleasure, amazement, reverence.

On the eighth day, I begin my period, go to bed early with wine and the vibrator. I alternate reading a science fiction story about a group of amazons and an erotic tale of two young women exploring each other's bodies. I buzz away with glee, forgetting the pain which only moments earlier had been my sole focus.

Each time I come, I relax for a while, return to the science fiction until the pain becomes insistent, then switch to the women and turn on the vibrator, pushing the pain back to a manageable level.

For two mornings I awaken groggy and slow. On the third, I have regained my clarity and celebrate, fingers in cunt again.

When Christine returns, I feel radiant. We make love before she unpacks, then lie on the bed, kissing, and catching up with the details of each other's lives.

☆ ☆ ☆

I injure my shoulder while splitting wood. It feels as if it is not sitting in its socket right. Lying on it feels like being poked by broken egg shells. I find myself aware of it constantly, incessantly. I visit a chiropractor who uses sonar on it and gives me some exercises to do. Neither seems to make very much difference. An M.D. gives me a prescription for pain killer and tells me not to strain it.

Sex becomes more difficult. When going down on Christine, I can't bear to brace on my elbows, so take to lying on my side between her legs, stroking her vagina and entranceway as my tongue flickers around her glans.

I begin using my left hand to make love to her instead of my right, always surprised and delighted when she comes from it. Sometimes I use my right hand, bracing my arm or wrist with my left.

Christine's good nature helps us through abrupt changes in position, gives me the courage to ask her to touch herself if the pain becomes too great for me to continue. Sometimes, I'll lie beside her, finger inside her vagina as she strokes herself into bliss.

71

"It feels like both of us making love to me," she says.

I decide to go swimming and visit a local spa with a large hot Jacuzzi next to a small warm swimming pool. I do very gentle warm-up exercises in the Jacuzzi which they call a rehabilitation pool, then swim breast stroke for several laps in the larger pool. I do this every evening.

Within a week, the pain in my shoulder is gone. In two weeks, I can do long strokes again. I luxuriate in the water, turning, surface diving, doing water ballet tricks when no one else is around. I love the water, feel it on my face, pressing in, sliding along my body, tingling cold when I change pools. I develop a routine wherein I swim two sets of laps, alternating with the hot pool, then sit in the redwood sauna for as long as I can tolerate the heat. In the sauna my mind seems to clear and dream outward. I imagine and plan for the days and weeks ahead, sift my possibilities, make choices.

One evening, even without my glasses on, I can tell that a lesbian couple have entered. They are being shown around by the attendant. I question myself about why I am sure they are coupled, something about their presence, the way they move their bodies. They return in bathing suits while I'm doing laps. I want to make contact, don't want to stare, find I'm swimming exceptionally well. Halfway through my last lap, I do a small, fancy dive, bubbling with exuberance. I hadn't realized how isolated I felt here with women talking about babies and grandbabies.

I smile at the couple as I switch into the hot pool. The butch, a classy-looking woman in her early fifties, returns my smile. Her lover, younger, less poised, glares.

"But I'm settled," I want to say. "I don't want your lover. Let's be friends."

I say nothing, retreat to a corner and do shoulder rotations.

The butch gets into the colder pool and swims with power and grace. Her lover stands stiffly, half out of the water, with what looks like a combination of yearning and hot desire. When they go to shower, I do the same, hoping there will be a chance to talk. One smile is all I get, then our paths fail to cross again.

When I go to use the hair dryer, the younger woman is looking grimly at her own reflection in the mirror, gives me the fish-eye when I open with a tentative grin. You're not going to keep your lady long with an attitude like that, I think.

When I tell Christine about the encounter, she bristles at my description of the butch, affirms the femme's hostility. "You'd be competition for anyone," she says.

I hug her to me with gratitude and love.

February

Springtime arrives with fog and rain punctuated occasionally by a spectacularly sunny day. Daffodils appear abruptly, tiny whites and giant yellows, doubles with labia-like convolutions, salmon-edged flowers with fiery centers.

Christine is busy with editorial work and gardening. I've been struggling with a photo essay, the completion of which is eluding me.

One night I work late in the darkroom. The essay images have finally begun to cohere.

I show Christine the photographs, tell her I plan to continue working. She responds to my excitement, caresses me, suggests we make love.

I panic. If I stop now I'll lose the thread of understanding which has begun to shape the work.

"I can't," I say. "I'll lose it."

Christine goes to bed alone, but lets me know she's unhappy.

☆ ☆ ☆

Christine's been mining her old journals for short story material, crafting vignettes and short tales out of one of her hotter passions. Usually, I can listen with dispassionate attention. Sometimes, though, I don't want to hear about this other woman, how good it was back then.

One day, I write a short piece about a former lover of mine.

"I don't want you writing about other women!" she says.

"But you've been writing for months about other women, other lovers," I remind her.

"I'll stop," she says.

STORY OF ANOTHER LOVER

She was breathtakingly beautiful, a charcoal smudge against the night: the dark hair, translucent face, purple-rimmed eyes.

There were times when I would lean against any support to seem calm in her presence: walls, of course, juke boxes, other people.

The first time we made love, I noticed the way she smelled, perhaps it was due to her diet. Her odor was gently barnyard, put me in mind of southern heat.

She was not moist, a dry lover, more passionate in shadowy clutches than ever when we had a bed. And yet the sex was satisfying, perhaps because I could always make her come.

She never complained, seemed almost complacent and lied.

I was never sure if she knew she lied or whether she believed what she said when she said it, then changed her mind and failed to tell me.

Her beauty kept me near her for a while, even after I understood her nature. I hated to lose the inspiration, the vision she drew forth from me.

After we separated, I would find a faint metallic taste on my tongue whenever I thought of her, which was seldom in the intervening years.

Ah, but the pictures I did of her, always young, classy punk, large knuckled hands that could give such pleasure, hanging, at rest. Those pictures live on, need no apologies, no explanations.

I read Christine the story one night in bed. After, she turns away from me, doesn't want to talk.

"Don't go away from me," I plead.

"I'm not," she says grimly.

The next afternoon, she asks me to read the story to her again. Tells me she likes it. Thinks it's well-crafted.

"I felt hurt by your reference to her hands, the pleasure they could give you."

"Her hands never took me the places yours do, and I would never have enjoyed living with her."

Later, kneeling beside the sofa, stroking the cat, I close my eyes, following the rhythm of her purring. I stroke her soft belly, massage under her chin, along her cheek bones, behind her ears, between her shoulder blades. Her kitty fur is soft, like the hair edging Christine's face. With both hands, I caress her rib cage, moving the loose skin, reaching under her arms.

The cat stretches, inclines her body to maximum sensation, opens and closes her eyes slowly. I rub my face against her tummy, nose to nose, cheek to ear.

Quietly (cat-like), Christine comes up behind me, reaches under my shift and fondles the cleft between my legs. Rotating against my glans, she opens my outer, then my inner lips. My humming blends with purring and I rub against the cat, the velvety couch.

Sitting beside me, Christine begins working my vulva with both hands, pressing the clitoral pedestal, circling my minor valley, lightly dipping inside, teasingly retreating and reaching in again.

Suddenly, she enters me quite deeply with one finger, maybe two. I gasp and squeeze down tightly around her, tipping my pelvis and pushing against her. She plunges briefly and withdraws, spreading my liquid in her wake. Lover, beloved woman, I moan, wiggle, tingle. She enters me again and thrusts fuckingly into my accepting, adoring interior. Gentle splashing sounds mingle with the purring, my labored breathing.

The kitty begins to rub her body against my face as Christine nudges my clothing higher, she begins kissing and nibbling my side, rubs her cheek against my bottom, spreads kisses across my back. Her tongue trails toward the crack in my ass, taps its way downward until I feel it hard and moist against my anus.

I crouch against the sofa, face against the kitty, my heart a thunder in my ears.

Christine's tongue probes my clenched muscle, darts, becomes seductive, soft, moulding along my contours. My legs are shaking now, liquid runs along their insides. I feel her fingers still inside me, tongue against my throbbing sphincter, thumb caressing with her tongue. The pressure of her thumb increases. Briefly, I hold out against her, then open to her surging, her desire.

Singing with sensation, I am coming quickly, loudly, grateful to my body, to her sensitive determination, celebrating my response and her demands.

When I turn to Christine, curl into her arms, collapse with her onto the floor, the light is fading. Have we really been here hours? The kitty climbs over my shoulder, snuggles into my lap.

March

We've been making love in the silvery early morning light. Resting now, she brings me coffee in bed. Cozy and warm, my fingers smell of sex each time I raise my cup. I pick up *WHAT LESBIANS DO*, begin to read aloud to her, a morning ritual of two, sometimes three, poems. Today I read from Marilyn Gayle's long piece called "Between Turns" which starts out:

> "Write about how I come," I urged her,
> because I like to read about myself
> look at pictures of myself
> reap attention of any kind
> and because I had come three times
> just previously
> colossally.

She rests her cheek against my thigh, her flesh opalescent. I think about the journals Christine's kept since the age of sixteen, about the growth and vitality contained in them. Humming I run my fingers through her hair where it mingles with my own.

I return to reading M. Gayle, who weaves the details of sex, daily living, psychic and emotional awareness into the fabric of her poem:

> We've gone so far
> as to move to separate houses
> because I went berserk, what can I say?
> and gave her a black eye for crowding me

or because I hadn't crowded her enough.
I hit her for my jealousy and hers.
Because of all the times she took her leave
of me and kept me near. Because
when she puts her face between my legs
she gets too close to me, time and again, and
crowded by her power over me
during each grudging surrender
I doubt my own motives
for putting myself through
these forbidden devastating bolts of pleasure.

Christine asks me to read more slowly, sometimes has me repeat a section or a line. I feel lightheaded with her presence, my own feelings of well-being. "Forbidden devastating bolts of pleasure" particularly excites me and I read it through several times, accenting it differently, spreading it out, rolling it. Return to "Between Turns":

I keep longing to start fresh, with
somebody new, with no accumulated grudges.
Other times I think my guilt and grudges
go with me no matter who I'm with.
Some women only beat around my bush, but she
has gotten close enough to make me fly up.
Or with her I let me fly
and she scares me when she makes me
show myself.

I think about long and short relationships; about keeping the emotional circuits clean versus hanging on to all the little and big hurts. A friend of mine often comments "shit fertilizes," another adds ". . . only when it's spread around."

In a brief relationship, I don't try to explain very much, enjoy the moments and leave the differences alone. When living with someone I seek out understanding, sometimes losing the larger patterns in my nearsighted attempt to reach consensus.

We've been discussing S&M lately, my distrust of the aspect of nastiness and humiliation that sometimes/often seems to accompany writings about it. I talk about the way restraint, biting and scratching are treated in the *KAMA SUTRA*, one of my early erotic texts. She is interested in my ideas, but plays devil's advocate, drawing me out. I tell her about reading *STORY OF O* when it first came out. How I'd never read anything like it before and found it wildly exciting. I would come home from work, strip and masturbate while reading it in the hot summer evenings. Years later in a discussion group, a woman talked about how the flagellation scenes had always turned her on. I had felt surprised at the time, realized I'd always skipped those, preferring the moments of public display and the quality of possession by another. Christine says that the religious substructure turned her on the most.

The following morning, she brings some old journals into the bedroom and reads me notations she made in the early seventies about *STORY OF O*. As I listen to her, I think it sounds like a totally different book from the one I remember. We laugh. I say that, perhaps, accounts for its continued popularity: the different levels it works on, the multiplicity of stories, the fact that it is a story within a story, the fantasy of a woman writing an erotic fantasy to turn her lover on.

☆ ☆ ☆

Waking slowly from an erotic dream, I turn to find Christine awake, already excited, waiting for me to join her. I run my hands along her soft torso, rub my face between her breasts. We roll over each other, laughing. Her feet cuddle mine, slide up and down my legs. I squeeze her bottom, her thighs, press my clitoris against her flesh-softened bones. I cherish this luxury of time.

The day is overcast. Ornamental cherries bloom outside the window. We've made the room inviting: fabric walls, furry bedspread, rugs. I'm nesting into her in the smaller and larger senses: her body, the room, our home. Contentment opens other doors in me.

She combs her fingers through my curling hairs still pressed between our bodies, moves, presses my thigh down with one knee. I expand, lift my mons, caress her cheek, beam mellow adoration from still sleepy eyes. She moulds my outer lips between her fingers, drawing a dull, aching longing from my body. I moan low and long, rub my breasts against her.

She begins kissing me, nibbling my lips, rubbing my nose with hers. I run my fingers through the hair over her ears, form little circles on her scalp, massage her neck. She presses the flat of her forearm against my cleft, rotates, nudges. Such pleasure she gives me.

She dips her fingers into my expectant wetness, slides one inside and slowly picks up speed. I blossom for her, open wider, rise to meet her, follow every nuance.

I dream out, feel myself a part of the larger world, unfold like springtime leaves. She varies the rhythm, attuned to my body's attention. I feather outward, drift with mists and clouds. She becomes demanding. My whole being quickens. Hard, her finger moves hard between my legs, pressing glans and inner walls, calling me to her, to my own strong need for release now bunching in my central core. I perceive myself filling with light, pulsing, yearning, gripped by a force that is clearly me yet not my conscious self. I coalesce around my own desire, then throw myself outward as the climax overtakes me, crying out in one, long descending howl.

I must have slept, wake to find myself a ball around her hand still buried in my body, touch her face with love. She asks if I want coffee, says she'll save her orgasm for later in the day. I do want coffee, am pleased by her attentions.

In the afternoon she comes to me horny, has completed a building project. We return to bed, she hurries me through the preliminaries of lovemaking, takes my hand and places it between her legs. Oh yes, wet. I go inside her with one, then two fingers, match my strokes to her breathing. She comes almost immediately in small, wavering spasms, wants more.

I circle her clitoris with light strokes, growing lighter till she comes again, this one large and hard, gripping me with legs and arms, singing her pleasure.

Subsiding, she wants me inside her again, just my presence, tells me not to move. She trances out for a while, returns to play and tease. Later we talk about our lovemaking, remembering, holding each other warm.

April

Friends are staying over for a week. One is allergic to corn and corn products. I start cooking everything from scratch, reading the details on labels, questioning the processing of each product. Preparing egg salad sandwiches for a picnic, I locate a recipe for making mayonnaise in a blender. The results are a vinegary goo and everyone gathers in the kitchen reading different cookbooks, trying to find out what went wrong. We decide that the quantities for vinegar and oil have been reversed, begin again. Laughing, everybody pitching in, chopping onions, shelling eggs.

In the morning we rise early and take my station wagon, driving through the dark woods, winding into snow. The vista we choose looks out over a lake, mountain-rimmed, turquoise, azure.

Clouds sweep past, gather, explode into a sudden storm filled with lightning and wind. We drop the back seat, spread the blanket and picnic in our private shelter.

Shortly, the storm passes and we explore again, Christine running in circles, arms outstretched, around the powdery field. I take off my sandals and socks, remove the loose slacks I have pulled over my shorts and run, barefoot, through the snow to leap into her arms. Our friends take pictures, cheer us on. Tourists gape or grin. The world seems lovely, rich and generous. I am so happy.

Returning, we talk about sex and power, pain and dreams. Christine says she sometimes worries when she fantasizes during sex, fears reality isn't good enough.

I draw on my fantasies like accomplices, sisters, drugs, watch them change from year to year. The happier I am, the richer and more varied my waking dreams become.

Cuddling in bed that night, Christine and I reflect upon the day, how good it feels to be ourselves, relax, sharing with others who are unravelling similar paths, related thoughts. I am brimming over, caress her in my joy, slowly, watching her become fluid, dreamy then searching, moist, vital, spume forth with pleasure, fizz, aerate. High with her excitement I touch myself, picturing her face, hearing again her sounds. She snuggles against me, sucks one breast, slides her finger in toward my womb. Awash in tingling sensations, I rub and sing a wordless song, praising my body and hers. Oh, comfort of recurring passion, effervescent love.

Part III:

Another Spring Will Follow

May

Via telephone, I learn that my most recent pap test shows a class four situation with severe dysplasia. The doctor does an examination using a microscope that allows him to observe the cervix more closely. He says that the abnormal cells go all the way inside the os, the opening to the uterus. I agree to having a conical section removed from my cervix and a D&C.

I enter the hospital in the early morning, return home after the surgery in the afternoon. Christine stays near me whenever she can. I feel sluggish, worried.

The lab reports from the two sets of tissue samples show that the abnormal development has spread throughout the uterus. This is still considered a precancerous condition but just barely. The doctor recommends a hysterectomy. At first I refuse, then late one night, decide to go ahead with the surgery. I am very frightened.

June

Christine drives me to the hospital. We're joking but it's not funny. I can't remember feeling such terror in my adult life.

Settling in my hospital room, I try to relax. There are so many details: people, questions, blood tests, explanations.

The surgery will take place early in the morning. Christine stays with me as long as she can.

I walk to the small chapel and meditate, read aloud from the Book of Ruth, ask for protection. I reach out for the ordering power of the universe, that which heals, fixes, straightens, restores balance.

After the surgery, I awaken to pain, and pain dominates the following weeks. Slowly my world enlarges; the healing overcomes distress.

July

Sarah always said orgasms felt different after her hysterectomy. That she remembered how her uterus would contract first, and now that was gone.

I'm leaning over Christine, who sits in front of her typewriter at her desk. She has turned sideways and is touching my arm and thighs very lightly, kissing me with lips gone soft and hungry the way hers can sometimes. I start to shake so we move to the bed. Her voice has become husky, surprisingly deep, a characteristic which always betrays her excitement, even when she tries to keep her cool.

She touches my arms again, my breast, slipping inside the kimono. My pelvis begins to reach for her rhythmically and I open to her, raising my leg and bracing my knee against the wall. Turning, she clasps my other leg tightly between hers and trails her fingers down the tube top I am wearing to support my tummy to where my fur is just beginning to grow in again. Slowly, with one finger, she traces firm little circles in the cleft of my mons. I begin to shake again and wedge my hips more firmly between her torso and the wall.

Her finger dips down lower and returns to my center all dewy and slick, making larger circles around the glans this time. She chuckles, as ever, at how wet I have become. Briefly I slip into one of my favorite fantasies. The one where we have been making love all night, she demanding that I come over and over in a variety of

ways — manually, orally, anally, touching and teasing
me for both our pleasures on and on until I move past
thinking, past my own vibrant will and sense of direction and simply follow her wherever she takes us.

I return to her staccato fingers tapping out the rhythm
of excitement between my legs now more intense after
each visit to the fantasy. Wonder how she can bring me
to this weightless golden yearning place over and over.
I want you, I repeat inside my head, I want you, make
me come. I want you, make me come. Outside my head,
I hear myself making little mewing, moaning sounds,
shift my hips again, move one arm so that both encircle
her neck, pull her to me even more.

Abruptly, I know I'm going to come, can't seem to
tell her, can't even say "Don't stop," am scared to arch
my back, scared to tense my newly healing stomach muscles, come so quietly I know she doesn't know I've come.
I tell her to move her fingers down to feel the spasms
and watch her face light up at that outward and visible
sign.

"Oh, good, you still work," she says.

"Were you worried I wouldn't?" I ask.

"Yes," she answers.

"Me, too," I say and snuggle into her neck to drift
and dream and remember.

Maybe I sleep a bit, then rouse to ask, "But what
about your orgasm?" meaning "Do you want to come?"
She says if I want her to she will. I want her to but
don't think I have the strength to make love to her.
"Would you touch yourself?" I ask, bemused to notice
she's still wearing her tee shirt and shorts. "Yes." She
wiggles around to free her other arm, free her torso from
the pants, closes her eyes. I pull myself across her breast,
brush her cheek, kiss her neck and cheek, lips, and hair.
I hold on more tightly as she starts to rock, then she
becomes a heaving ship and I am clinging to the mast
until the storm is over.

"I love you," she says.

"Me, too," I say before I drift away.

☆ ☆ ☆

In the heat of the next afternoon, I am lying on the sofa bed wearing only the purple tube top around my hips and stomach; reading. She sits down to talk about dinner and almost casually touches me there, between my legs. I come instantly alive to her and we both grin. Almost clinically she examines my labia, touching, always touching. "We could . . ." I say. "Mummmm . . ." she says and climbs onto the bed, straddling my leg. I unzip her shorts and reach inside but the angle's wrong so content myself with sliding my fingers under the bottom edge of her pants, up and down her thigh.

My passion is building quickly as she continues stroking, pulling, her eyes watching first her fingers, then my face. I imagine that I have taken some powerful drug and my body is relaxing totally; worry, tensions, pain all swept away leaving me caught in some eternal present, all my senses intensified. I squeeze her breast with one hand and pinch my own nipple with the other, delighting in the ripples of excitement this sends speeding to my cunt, speeding to her movements there.

My focus gathers, tightens and then falls away once, twice. I remind myself not to become frightened: sooner or later I will come, by her hand or my own. She keeps wetting her fingers and moving them across my inner lips in wide broad sweeps. I take short, rapid breaths, relax, hyperventilate, start to climb my green, glowing mountain once again.

Deep inside I feel the clutching of a big one coming, the sensation I thought I might have lost. I let it rise gingerly, not wanting to grab at it, letting the ingathering take its own time and path until I hear myself howling loudly, become pure sound: unlovely, raw, scraping my throat as it shatters around us both and I find my body again, shaking, clinging to her; very close to tears.

Later I tell her that if my response isn't really quite the same as it used to be, I can't tell the difference. She beams at me and says that Gertie, our yellow lab, turned over and sighed deeply when I came.

While cuddling I have an intense desire to stretch lengthwise and go down on her. I laugh at myself: my mobility is still severely limited. I can't lie on my stomach even for short periods of time. I decide to ask her if she will move to the edge of the bed, let me try kneeling on the floor between her legs. She looks dubious but removes her pants and slides to the foot of the bed, making me promise that if anything hurts in me, I will stop immediately and let her finish herself.

I spread a skirt on the rug and drop a small pillow on top of it. Kneeling, I move carefully from side to side, forward and back. I ask her to move a few inches more into the bed so that my rib cage is comfortably supported, my lower torso unencumbered. I look down at her soft golden nest and feel again that awe that overcomes me at the sight of so much beauty blooming there.

Dipping my face close, I lick my fingers and separate her folds, take in that truly heady perfume. Spreading her lips with my tongue, I explore for momentary responses, places where her pleasure rises to the surface. Sliding my arms around her thighs I readjust my position and relax into meditative, flowing movements with my head, tongue nudging her clit, pushing against the hood. Her pelvis sets the tempo, comes to meet me faster now, faster. She is very hot today.

I remind myself that I'm the one who's hurt, not her. I need not hold back for her sake. I increase the stimulation, tucking upper lip over teeth and pressing down on the shaft just north of her glans. She begins to toss from side to side. I know she's coming now, settle to a steady motion, attending to not changing speed or direction.

Wildly, she begins to peak. I hold her thighs to me tightly since I cannot follow her across the bed. She clasps my head with her soft legs, cutting off my hearing of her sounds. Relaxing some, "Enough," she says, still rising to my tongue. "Enough, I can't take any more." I climb onto the bed beside her, pulling a knitted rug across our bodies for security as much as warmth.

Languidly she takes my hand, peers at the shortness of the nails and places my fingers at the entrance to her womb. I drift awhile, touch recent moments in my mind, then contract my fingers in a pulsing movement. She thrusts against me gently, then stops my motion, saying she doesn't want to come again just yet. I rest, fingers inside her, until a different kind of hunger moves us both.

☆ ☆ ☆

Christine starts her period. I bring her hot water bottles, tea, wine, take care of her today. Think about never having monthly pains again. No more blood on the sheets.

In the evening I climb into bed early. She asks if I mind if she uses the vibrator for an orgasm to relax her, relieve the cramps. I don't mind, wiggle against her, remember times we've played with the knob-tipped wand together, finding positions where we could share the stimulation, laughing, trying to come at the same time. Now she hums and buzzes along, crests quickly and then seems to melt, her body so soft beside me. She holds me in her arms as we both enter sleep.

In the morning, when she mentions the vibrator, I remember only the sound of music, her body rocking, her voice calling out in joy and release.

One afternoon I cut the firethorn back, reshape the bush away from my studio window, relish being out of doors.

Waking, I find I've done too much. Was it the sex? The gentle working out of doors? I spend a couple of days in bed, pain and sleep, fighting off a cold.

Feeling better, I write about our lovemaking, what we did and how we came. When I read this to her, she says it turns her on. I tell her my pain went away completely while I was writing but now it has returned. Climbing under my blanket she asks if sex would distract me from the pain. I say I think I hurt too much to respond but she says no, she meant she wanted to masturbate and should she go away or do it with me. I warn her that I may dash to the toilet any minute. She reassures me and unfastens her soft blue pajamas, pulls the blanket over both our heads.

I part the robe her grandmother gave her, to gain access to her pliant, rich breasts and rub them through the flannel, feel the nipples harden and push back. She looks so much like the *Shunga* prints I have been studying, draped in layers of cloth with only her tummy, curling fur and bent wrist showing. I feel better, settle against her shoulder, relax into the homey smells.

Her hand between her legs quickens. Her breath catches, comes in little gasps. I stroke her and croon to her, caught up in the power of her concentration, of her expanding joy. She moans. Rocking, she moans louder. I take a firmer hold upon her breast and press against her as her orgasm spreads in ripples of movement and musical sound. "I love you," I chant. "I love you. I love you."

☆ ☆ ☆

Days pass and the pain continues to recede. My walks become longer. A night comes when I can sleep on my side without holding a pillow against me.

One afternoon I am lying on my side drifting in and out of memories/sleep. Earlier, I had considered masturbating, scanned my turn-on shelf: two by Anais Nin, WHAT LESBIANS DO, MY SECRET GARDEN, SHARED INTIMACIES; decide to wait for Christine.

Christine returns and crawls into bed behind me. Luxuriantly, I shift from my reveries to her caresses, murmurs of love. Leaning over me she defines my ear with her tongue. I make small, encouraging sounds and she moves farther into the interior, circling, twining, touching. My other ear is buried in the pillow, so all sound is distanced as she reaches in.

I imagine that I am fourteen, that she is an older girl I have a crush on who is teaching me about pleasure. She begins to tongue my ear with rapid, fucking movements. I am squeezing my legs together, sending streaks of delight radiating up my torso, down my legs. She presses my nipple repeatedly between her fingers, intensifying the almost unbearable sensations.

I tell her I am going to touch myself and begin to do so, finding my clit enlarged and throbbing, nether lips all swollen. She spreads oil on her fingers and slides one into my bottom. I feel like exploding with all the tingling, jangling everywhere in my body as she plunges her finger deep inside me, in and out, in and out. My orgasm comes rushing at me quickly, taking my outer edges first, moving in waves toward my center.

Lazily I turn over, trail my fingers down her body through her curls to check the wetness of her inner lake. Swimming there awhile, I pull the liquid up around her glans, stroking her shaft. Lighter, ever lighter I move, breaking contact then returning, dipping, stirring, make her reach out just a little, make her wait just a little, slow and patient, swoop and touch, hold and touch, rub and wait.

Dreamily, I follow as her body moves toward my flying, fleeing, tapping fingers, steady now, steady up the beat and hold the rhythm steady till she comes. "I'm coming," she says. "I'm coming." And she does with streams of little "oh" sounds, her body arching up and back then, flowing down and shivering, she pulls me to her tightly, squeeze, squeeze. Still dreamy, I nuzzle at her shoulder, nudge my head against her neck.

Half asleep I tell her how, before the surgery, I was so scared sex would feel different in some major way that I decided not to even think about it, much less talk about it with her. She hugs me, tells me she understands.

October

Autumn moves lazily across the land. Maples turn yellow near the water, aspen gold, dogwood flecked with pink. Poison oak drapes embankments in a bright, ravishing scarlet. The leaves fall, alder, ash, oak, gather in piles against the bushes and buildings, cover bridges, clog the creek. Acorns grow large, bang on the roof as the wind shakes them free.

Pain is now a memory but I still tire easily. Christine stacks the winter wood.

Periodically, Christine and I have fought. Sometimes now, we stalk the house angry, not speaking. Healing comes slowly, sorting out past histories, present needs. I learn that when angry and hurt, I often react with sarcastic phrases. She feels attacked by these, does not understand my pain, withdraws. I panic, needing her to hold me, yet pushing her away. The child in me is cold and scared. We work at our disagreements like puzzles, sometimes more, sometimes less successful.

At times she says she's leaving and I half want her to go. Resolutions are not predictable. Is this a stage of growing closer too?

☆ ☆ ☆

Christine sleeps late this morning. I caress her long, slumbering body, then dress and go outside. I take one of the logs we've had cut for seating around the fire pit and begin rolling it down the slope toward the creek.

One end is enough larger than the other that it constantly careens to the side.

The second log I choose for its symmetry and it rolls easily. I think about learning activities and how the first is often the hardest, the one I learn the most from.

As I dig out the pit, I transfer the grass to barren patches along the edge of the creek. Later, I light a fire to "Bitterness," naming the bundles of briers after people with whom I have fought. I think about the holding on and letting go of anger as the flames embrace the thorny branches. Small explosions spit out from slate chips I have accidentally gathered with the pebbles and rocks.

As the flames quiet, I carry bucket after bucket full of water, soaking the embers until charred pieces float.

☆ ☆ ☆

One afternoon, Christine and I walk to the fire pit with its two upright log seats. She suggests that we have a ritual burning of our troubles.

We gather a water bucket, candles, and paper to light frosty blackberry canes. Lighting the candles first, we then use them to light the paper. I feel very close to her. Sad, too, that so much loving can include so much anguish.

Christine places a moss-covered branch on the fire and names it "The Letting Go of Past Things Even if They Are Attractive, if They Come Between Us."

She names a thick blackberry cane "The Getting Rid of Old Prickles in Order to Have the Berries."

I gather and burn leaves, naming them the words that I have used to separate us.

We encourage the fragile fire with dried grasses, more blackberry canes, old clippings, dead twigs, and branches. The fire sputters and grows, sending embers high, warming us. Adding larger and larger branches, we talk as honestly, as truthfully, as we can.

Some things we just don't understand, don't have words to name.

The fire holds steady for a long time, then drops and dies. We watch until it's coated with ash and the wind reaches inside our clothes.

Reluctantly, we wet the fire and return to the house, arm in arm, talking. I look at her face, so dear and fine, and treasure this moment of peace and closeness.

☆ ☆ ☆

We decide to practice the fox trot for a dance being held in a city about an hour's drive away. One particular Joan Baez song delights us and we play it repeatedly, perfecting our turns and breaks.

We dress with care for the dance itself. I'm long and elegant, she's all soft and velvet-blazered. The DJ waves to us as we enter. I'm pleased to see who's spinning the tunes. She'll play some slow ones especially for us. The crowd of women is electric.

Between dances, we visit with friends, try out new steps, dance with other women.

As I look around the room, I'm reminded of the first women's dance I ever went to, ten years ago in a small, chilly warehouse: wall-to-wall women, smiling. I had recently left my husband. My friend's lover had run off with someone else. She and I often danced together at women's bars in those years. She knew where the bars were and I had a car and enthusiasm. There we'd be in our long dresses, she'd be leading on the fast numbers and I would lead on the slow ones. My mother would be surprised at the uses to which I've put my dancing lessons.

Later in bed, I feel as if Christine and I are still dancing. She holds me firmly, leading with conviction. I respond with fervor, attentive to her every nuance. She showers me with adoration. I glitter with enthusiasm. She pursues me with ardor. I acquiesce with charm, lightly veiling my excitement. The pleasure of my coming bubbles over us like the music. Her sympathetic contractions, encouraged by my fingers, draw us both together for a whirling finale, music echoing in our ears.

Here in the arms of this shimmering, lovely woman I relax, believe in the rightness of the two of us together, believe, passionately, that we can find our way.

November

It's storming outside, rain slamming against the windows, branches hurled across the yard.

We have a huge fight beginning innocuously enough with my not wanting to make love when she does. Everything each of us says is the wrong thing to say. She begins to pack to leave. I am angry, tearful, vengeful. She is coldly silent, tight, pinched: face white, brow furrowed, eyes round.

We fight violently, physically, painfully. Afterward, we comfort each other, cry together, sleep entwined, curled into a tight little ball. The rain continues all night long.

In the morning we make love, straighten the house, review the evening, decide to get professional help in working through our difficulties.

Touching her, I feel safe. Sometimes, when alone, I fear the return of the angry stranger in her.

☆ ☆ ☆

We arrange to spend two weekends in group therapy marathons with a couple of family counselors who have helped me through difficult times before. While there, we frequently find ourselves dealing with childhood hurts and fears that we have been bringing, not always appropriately, into our present lives.

Returning home we take back roads, winding through open fields and misty forests. For a brief time we travel along the coast, stop to walk along the shore. Christine wants to run, so disappears into the distance, playing tag with the waves. I gather rocks into a series of small altars, sequential holy places. The ocean was my childhood concept of God, of that which was holy. It was both always present and constantly changing, life-supporting, rich beyond imagining. The child in me is still in awe of it, the adult feels renewed by it. I dig my toes into the sand, savor the smells.

I'm reminded of Gray Scameron's poem "I Walk On God":

> I walk on God
>   She is the Earth
> I wade in God
>   She is the Ocean
> I inhale God
>   She is the Air
> I bask in God
>   She is the Sun
> I glimpse God
>   She is the creatures
>   of the Earth
> I am in awe of God
>   She is the Universe
> I am God
>   She is Me.

I stand a line of bird feathers upright in the sand, place a heart-shaped rock at one end whispering "I love you, Christine. I love you, Christine."

The wind begins to turn chill and I walk off in the direction Christine took some hours ago. Soon, a dim figure emerges from the haze, running, almost in slow motion. I set a steady pace and soon recognize her clothing, then her smile and I'm enveloped in her exuberance.

Returning to our car we hold hands, beam at the gulls, point out figurations that catch our interest. We spend the night in a chilly motel, spreading our sleeping bags on top of the covers to increase the warmth. We make love dreamily, almost but not quite coming several times. We drift off, wrapped in each other's arms, comforted. Tomorrow may open up more problems. Tonight is gentle with love.

Cream

A Suite of Thirty-one Erotic Poems

CREAM

1.
Pubo-
coccy-
geal
Muscle
Tightening, squeezing,
Claiming my fingers
for your pleasure.

2.
Eating out
eating in
eat me now
here
no one will come by.
I want you
want to give myself to you
want to release us both
from this high, tingling excitement.

3.

Creamy, creaming
slippery, running
love liquid, wild honey
glides downward
toward the cleft in your bottom:
    curves
    crevices
    rivulets
    spent lubrication.

4.

Fingering your pearl, your hidden lady,
I am transported
touch you
as I would touch myself.

5.

Come, let us love fiercely now
together again, however briefly.
Let me bury my face
in your sweet golden nest.

6.

The curl of your underarm hair
delicate rib cage, prominent mound.
Dear love, let me treasure the moment.
Your body lit from the side
My desire rising once again.

7.
You lie on top of me
humping me
pressing against me.
So perfectly matched these
vulval mountains move
in intricate patterned circles
radiating joy.

8.
How can I come again
want you again so
quickly after you
brought me to a
howling, intense
conclusion?

9.
Deep inside of me
I feel your fingers plunge
hear the sound of oceans'
liquid splashing at my shore.
Rising, I push to meet you
responding, my ocean to your moon.

10.
You taste so sweet, lemon fresh,
spread beneath my nose.
I tongue your avocado smoothness,
finger the soft peach inside.

11.

I cover you with almond oil
long strokes, praising your
body, questing your hollows
firing then filling, desire.

12.

Blood everywhere, my face and fingers,
the sheets. Oh but we've
had a lovely time, affirming
fertility, easing cramps
enjoying life.

13.

Suckling one breast,
squeezing the other
I fondle you as you
initiate your own pleasure.

14.

Delicately you finger my bottom,
flutter your tongue across
my glans.
Springtime . . . I flower for you

15.

Lie back now, well fed, read to,
let me tickle your fancy
touch your labia
excite your inner lake.

16.

Your pubic hair foams
in the morning light.
My fingers swim in it
after and before delight

17.

Your bottom above my face
your lips caressing my nether ones
Magic of electric surges
toes tingling, nipples erect, spasms
mine? yours?
Bodies slick and rich with smells.

18.

I dream we're making love,
wake to kiss and slide against you.
Domestic Bliss I call it.
Bliss, you say, just bliss

19.

Springtime returns daily
when you touch me
there and there.

20.

Reaching between our bodies
I caress your vulva, moist
with expectation.

21.

The sound of your coming echoes
muffled by your thighs
against my ears.

22.

The pleasure of our friendship
deepens the communion of our bodies,
softens the primitive in our love.

23.

Kissing, soft lips, full mouth,
pressing face to face
touching downy cheeks, cornsilk hair.

24.

I am so hot for you
quivering with passion intensified
by separation.
Come, hold me here, touch me here.
Let me feel you inside me once again.

25.

Legs pulled against my chest
toes curling
carpopedal spasms
myotonia: sexual tension
twitching, quaking
fingers knotted
into balls behind my knees.
How long can I endure
this riot of sensation?
Delay,
delay.

26.

Orgasm, coming, climax
dynamite, yes, summation.

27.

Coming, quietly, gently,
wind in poplar trees.

28.

The little girl in you
emerges from your sleep.
Voluptuous after coffee
you expand, hot, eager
fully in heat.

29.

Sunlight wraps around your body
drops of water and goosebumps
speckle your skin.
Me, I want to grab you,
warm you from the inside out.

30.

Coming,
small wonders,
everyday miracles.

31.

It's the daily loving, the good sex,
snuggling in sleep, cooking together,
that make me want
to continue
at your side.

Dreams of the Woman
Who Loved Sex

The Woman in Love was born in the mind of a quiet, lonely child whose heart was fed on family tales, southern songs and country/western music. Moving in three-quarter time, she spun her dreams of an active, vibrant life, layering the images, the smells, across her senses. She watched her mother with the magnificent breasts, her gypsy aunt and stately mother's mother. She loved them with a deep and colorful passion. Their perfumes filled her world long after they had left for one party, event, meeting or another. She would hold a glove or stole against her face, breathe deeply and slip into a dream of beautiful, graceful women who always had time to spend with her.

The Woman in Love grew amid the Spanish moss, century plants, dogwood, magnolia, orange and grapefruit trees.

The lush, moist heat nourished her, wrapped around her, insulated her, caressed her incessantly, fed and satisfied her dreams. The sun darkened her lean body, warmed the sand and water, created mirages that glittered in the distance on the midday roads.

Her world was filled with flowers: gardenias, bougainvillaeas, hibiscus, jacarandas, frangipanis, fragrant, intensely colored. The women cultivated flowers, wore them, taught her their secrets and their names.

Always skinny, she ate for the sensuous pleasure food afforded, ate to fill a variety of hungers, ate pecans and peaches brought down from Georgia, figs, peanuts from her grandmother's garden, coconut milk, sweet-potato pie, avocado from the tree out back, hush puppies made from corn meal and minced onion, deep-fried, crispy on the outside, warm and steamy on the inside.

Holidays were filled with chicken dusted in flour and fried, roast turkey, leg of lamb, fresh oysters, chicken livers with thick white gravy, sauteed onions and spiced apple sauce.

Her family ate well, fished, grew, gathered, canned, smoked, fermented and drank their way through the years of her childhood. They died off quickly in her youth, leaving her rich with memories.

Out of the dreams and memories, she fashioned a life that satisfied the longings of the child that she had been and the woman she was rapidly becoming. She grew willowy and serene, fell in love with butchy, androgynous women, queer like herself, traveled and talked and rubbed against them in the warm nights of Mobile, Charleston, Savannah, St. Augustine.

☆ ☆ ☆

Oh, seduction, that glorious ephemeral art of attraction, the drawing of one individual to, toward, into another's sphere. The Woman in Love thrived on seduction: intellectual, aesthetic, visceral. She loved meeting people, unraveling their stories, learning who they were and are.

Sometimes she was seduced by others: the way one moved her body, the turn of a head or phrase, the revealing of an exquisite piece of work. At times she was seduced by those who unveiled only hints of themselves, knowing the fragments would lure her. Usually these women did not remain to become her friends. More often she would be drawn to those who opened themselves to her, unfolding their passions, uncovering their goals.

Seduction: the art of letting another know who you are.

"Will you dance with me?" the other asked, knowing the Woman in Love melted into music. "Will you dance with me?" she said, meaning "Come and get to know me. Let me show you who I am." The Woman In Love moved into her arms, lightly touching, felt the music enter her like water, enter her like wine. Part of her knew this was no ordinary dance, knew as soon as the other's rhythm immediately matched, mirrored, found her own. They danced like liquid contained in a single glass, merging, swaying, hearts soaring until the music's end.

For the Woman in Love, seduction had begun early: noticing people notice her, a lover whose eyes followed her legs, a breath inhaled with the contact between eyes, a shoulder brushed by lips. The Woman in Love adored being touched, fondled her own being, rubbed and hugged her friends. Sometimes, excited by the spirit of life itself, the Woman in Love would hold anyone in order to anchor herself to the maiden earth, grounding renegade energy racing through her torso. She knew no other way to channel her own electricity, to keep herself from turning into pure spirit, losing contact with others, with any outside world. At times people she touched in this way thought the Woman in Love was coming on to them, expressed disappointment when the surface contact satisfied her needs.

The other drew the Woman in Love into her arms where she breathed deep and slow so as not to cry out in her joy. For this night the other's name was Desire and her flame engulfed them both. The Woman in Love gave her lips, her mouth to the other, raised her nipples to the other's hands. She raised her mons to the other's pubic bone, the other's leg sliding through, between her own. Desire held them, drove them, rousing cravings that could not be stilled. Desire took the Woman in Love, took her with a finality that was open-ended, nourishing,

115

invigorating. The Woman in Love curled around her lover, tensed and came, tensed and came.

Seduction: opening herself to another, allowing her hunger, her vulnerability to be known.

"Loving," she said, "always comes as a surprise, like the sunrise, even though I know it's going to happen over and over again; it always takes my breath away, opens up my memories of what is holy."

☆ ☆ ☆

Soft vibrations of the music, flashing jukebox lights, glitter, pulse, bang along her spine. Her clit, enlarged, demanding, cries out for attention, presses against her jeans, the chair, Desire's leg. They dance dirty, standing in one place, grinding their pubes against each other's thigh. The Woman in Love breathes with the bass line, undulates, inhales the other's musk.

In the street the night is hot, a doorway near, the other's breath in her ear another kind of music, the other's need, the hand inside her pants, the reaching, raging breath. The nearby music still propels her, hungry, open, wet and wanting only to be taken, only to be freed.

The Woman in Love first encountered Desire in New Orleans in the form of an elegant butch with beautiful bones. Neither tall nor short, exquisitely proportioned, Desire, with her almost boy's body, claimed her with hips and loving hands, knelt between her legs, breathing in all her secret places, touching her in the twilight, in the half-light, late into the mornings, quietly in corners, on half-deserted streets. Desire's tapered, neatly clipped fingers stirred a longing in the Woman in Love, made her restless, dissatisfied with even that which Desire gave.

Yet music opened the doors within the Woman in Love as she moved into Desire's arms, swaying slightly. Music sent out her butterscotch slow fingers and Desire took the Woman in Love, again and again. Was the night enough? Would any night be enough?

"I will give you this lifetime," the Woman in Love said, knowing she had even more to give. "I will give you this night, this day, for as long as love is green, fresh with new growth."

"Hold me tight," said Desire. "Need me hard."

☆ ☆ ☆

The Woman in Love met Desire in the French Quarter, at a party, with wine and cheese and art. Desire sat at the distant end of the courtyard, wearing white: hat, slacks, jacket, shirt open at the neck. The shadows both illuminated and obscured her. She smoked, gestured lazily, sipped a tall, frosted drink. Delicate, graceful women came and went from where she lounged, casual, observant.

The Woman in Love saw Desire as if from a long way off, down a tunnel, under water, like a beacon glowing in the shelter of the late afternoon.

"Who's that woman?" she asked her friends.

"Stay away from her, honey," the first replied. "She's trouble. Too smart for her own good."

"Too hot for her own good, you mean, don't you? Women always leaving their men for her, even when she doesn't want them."

"Right. She's not interested in settling down. Not that one. She's a writer, a Yankee, a reporter. Works for the Times-Picayune. Supposed to be from a good family. They pay her to stay away. You know the kind."

The Woman in Love didn't know, had never met the likes of her before but was certain, at that moment, that she wanted to know her, know more about her, touch and kiss and hold that lean, fine-boned body against her own.

The Woman in Love moved to the brightly lit portico and stood where her profile could be observed as she studied the paintings hanging there. She stood, hoping to be noticed, tingling with anticipation, expectancy. Someone brought her a drink. An old love lightly kissed her neck in passing, told her she looked beautiful. Having lost herself in conversation, The Woman in Love's awareness would return abruptly to the hazy white figure moving, ever closer, at the edges of her vision.

The Woman in Love's heart beat loudly as Desire moved near, touched her shoulder lightly and asked, in a voice felt before it was heard, "Would you like to dance?"

The room shivered. "Magic," the Woman in Love thought. "Magic is very near."

"Yes, thank you, I'd love to dance." The Woman in Love turned and faced Desire for the first of many times. She faced the woman's angular face and steady, sweet eyes. An explosion of spices, remembered pleasures, filled her mouth.

Desire brushed a lock of hair from the forehead of the Woman in Love, leaving the ghost of her fingers lingering, pulsing. Desire's hand, warm, settled at the Woman in Love's waist, gently guiding her through the foyer, among the other guests, the potted palms and ferns, the fringed and shaded lamps.

Finding a room where dancers swayed to recorded music, Desire opened her arms and the Woman in Love stepped forward, sliding one hand around Desire's neck, another settled in her outstretched hand. The Woman in Love was aware of her own breathing, the other's warmth, many perfumes like blooming flowers, cinnamon, the heavy thudding music, her nipples hardening against fabric, the subtle give of the other's breasts, Desire's cheek moving against her own.

"You smell like the women in Paris," Desire said.

"Chanel No. 5. An old lover sends it every year, perfume and chocolates and roses for my birthday."

"Are roses your favorite flower?"

"No, gardenias."

They circled and turned, broke for drinks, returned to dance close, their heat rising. The Woman in Love shook a little in her excitement, thinking, "This is too fast, too much. I'm not sure I'm ready for her, for pas-

118

sion or love, attraction or lust to pull me from my work.''
She imagined herself consumed by flames.

"I saw your paintings in the front room,'' Desire said.
"*Grief* and *Summer*. I liked them very much.''

"Thank you,'' the Woman in Love said, lowering
her head, remembering the oil of a woman dressed in
black, her mother, raging at death that stole her dreams,
that soon would steal her life. The Woman in Love
thought more thankfully of the second painting, *Summer*,
women lovers with flowers in their hair.

"I've seen your work before,'' Desire said, touching
the Woman in love's chin, drawing her back to the party.
"At the James Gallery. A large oil of a woman reading,
two women on a bench, some self-portraits.''

The Woman in Love stopped dancing, pleased and
startled. She smiled fully into the face of Desire, into
Desire's eyes.

"You mentioned Paris. Have you been there?'' the
Woman in Love asked.

"Yes.''

"To the Louvre?''

"Yes.''

"Is the *Winged Victory* as beautiful as photos make
her seem?''

"Yes. Very grand and sexual.''

"Maybe I'll visit her someday.'' The Woman in Love
felt shimmery, noticed the smell of cloves, of paprika,
of steamed bay leaves.

They danced several slow final turns of the room
before the Woman in Love decided to leave, wanting to
think, to savor the remembering, to catch her psychic
breath, to reconstruct her understanding of her self.

They wove a trail between friends and strangers, working slowly through the amber light, intimate odors, car-
damom and mint, Desire's hand resting lightly on the
Woman in Love's hip.

At the door they exchanged addresses, phone numbers, agreed to meet again, perhaps later in the week. Desire held the hand of the Woman in Love for a long time, studying her as if she were a work of art. Desire lifted the fingers of the Woman in Love and pressed them to her lips, that old engaging gesture.

"I'm being courted," the Woman in Love thought, "and I am charmed."

The kiss dissolved. They said goodbye. The Woman in Love walked toward the river feeling the evening full along the close-walled streets. She smelled the red bean and rice smells, the gumbo and crab, crawdaddy and shrimp. Jasmine bloomed. Somewhere a tenor sax slipped along the hot, damp, slow-moving air. She felt at home here, listened to scattered, distant conversations, music from the strip joints, barkers' calls mingling with the chatter of tourists, sailors whistles, horns tooting, laughter, a lean fiddler playing a high, wailing, cajun tune.

Before returning home she stopped for coffee, chickory spiced, light with cream. She ate bignettes, the light pastries dissolving against her tongue. Absently she licked the powdered sugar from one finger after another, thinking of the way Desire had kissed her hand, the feel of her cool lips, warm breath. She remembered Desire's hand, light and firm against her back, leading her. Thrill and fear seemed poised, balanced.

She went home, pushed through the wrought iron gate, crossed the narrow, bricked courtyard and climbed, dreaming, to the third floor. Lingering outside her door, she leaned against the balustrade, shook her head to clear and settle thoughts which drifted out across the tree-tops and into lighted rooms where a voice behind her shoulder asked, "Do you want to dance?"

Taking a deep breath, the Woman in Love acknowledged that she had run from Desire. Turning she entered her nest, dropped her clothes into the hamper, crawled between old and loving sheets and reached for her groin.

"I want her," she thought. "Want her," she sang quietly as her fingers worked their magic, her hips began to roll, her back to arch.

"Want her, want her," as she slowed rushing excitement, prolonged imminent joy.

At dawn, Desire knocked on her door, smiling ruefully, holding a gardenia.

"I couldn't sleep," she said.

They lay together late into the day. Desire held the Woman in Love. They held each other, rocking, talking, the sheets electrified, their hair in disarray.

They held each other that day and for many nights thereafter. Desire touched the Woman in Love demandingly, with leg and hands and tongue. The air filled with drifting odors: nutmeg, garlic, lemon, mustard, licorice, molasses, thyme.

In quiet times the Woman in Love thought, "Somehow, surely, this will enrich my work, will resonate in depth through all my future imagery. Please."

At other times she didn't think at all.

"Run off with me," the Woman in Love begged and Desire refused, following her own road into the future.

"I'll forget you," threatened the Woman in Love, but she never did.

The Woman in Love married for sex and comfort and shortly began taking lovers: women and very young men. Her husband adored her, drew life from the fires that burned within her, loved her genius for creative solutions.

"They say my father could repair a car with a hairpin," she would say, but of course that didn't explain her abilities. For generations, though, her family had been good with their hands.

Safely married, obsessed by the past, the Woman in Love began painting the hands of Desire, working sometimes from memory, sometimes from photographs. Although many of the canvases were realistically rendered, some were colored by passion: green in the shadows, brilliant reds, purples, cadmium edges.

☆ ☆ ☆

Exhausted, in the late afternoon, the Woman in Love dreams she's weaving through bamboo forests, toes squishing in warm mud, wandering among the eucalyptus, sniffing, open mouthed, inhaling, running through fields of mint: peppermint, gingermint, Egyptian mint, spearmint, apple mint, catnip, lemon balm, pennyroyal.

She runs, the Woman in Love dreams, running, smelling, embracing odoriferous day.

As evening comes over her, it overcomes her, lowering her onto soft plants, crushed leaves oiling her body. She lifts her hips into the face of evening, combing her fingers through her own hairs, claiming her pleasure in her womanly birthright, exposed, exalted, understood.

Awaking slowly to the entering evening, the Woman in Love runs her hands over her own body, reclaiming the real from the dream. Conscious now, she remembers the hands of Desire, inhales slowly, feeling the cool hands move over her, another awakening, memory encoded in all her surface cells.

☆ ☆ ☆

The lips of the woman behind the podium are pursed, full, generous, contained. The Woman in Love watches them forming vowels, articulating intricately structured thoughts, finely woven ideas.

Later those same lips, that same neat, sturdy body, magic persona across the table, those same lips eat chicken, salad, mashed potatoes, beans, mushrooms, eggs. The Woman in Love savors every movement, the gloss of oil, a crumb removed.

A social gathering this time, someone introduces them unnecessarily, but the act pleases the Woman in Love. They talk, watching each other's lips, against the glass, crackers, cheese, olives, nuts, marinated artichoke hearts. She imagines the woman's sensuality centered in those lips, breath crossing them, words crossing them, her own coming to them.

In her sleep, the Woman in Love dreams of those lips caressing her own, molding her breasts, parting and squeezing her labia. The lips and the matron who possesses them become for her the symbol of a sexuality that can survive time, culture, education. Her response to them is intense, explosive, flowering, extenuated.

Hot like a dry summer afternoon, she melts beneath those lips, quivers within them.

Waking, she wonders if there's any basis for her dream.

☆ ☆ ☆

The matrix of the dream lies in the vision behind her eyes, the sense of touch magnified exquisitely. Sometimes the dream has taste and smell, rarely words.

She braids the dreams, layers them, embroiders them, saves them for moments that seem to lack vision. She pulls them down like curtains against boredom, against unpleasant realities.

Sometimes she harvests the dreams like condiments, wallows in a multitude of them, prism-like, light-filled, splattering rainbows across the borders of her psyche.

Dreams, she says, are a richness no one can take away. She's heard that sleeping pills cause one to stop dreaming so she never takes them. Drugs she finds physically uncomfortable, their artificially induced dreams inferior to her own.

Sexuality flows through and from her like an underground river. She looks genteel, remote. Dancing though, dancing releases her. She moves into her body, becomes essential music flowing into the arms of any partner, any passing stranger, beloved friend, committed mate. See her move now, flashing sparks, waves of laughter warming up the room as she slips into the dream.

☆ ☆ ☆

Beloved fingers, spread across blue denim, flat against the table, felt at night, unseen; the Woman in

Love recalls the hands of Desire, longs for them, ripens for them. *She dreams she is a fruit tree within the beloved's land, an apple tree, pruned, cleaned of parasites, rich with fruit turning bright in the summer heat. She dreams her feet are roots sunk deep, drawing water from the unseen stream.*

Her only need in life is to ripen, to grow, sustain, survive. The beloved's fingers move over her, caress her bark, remove dead branches, leaves.

The tree of the Woman in Love sways in a lazy breeze, glistens with morning dew, traps moonlight in her veins. She sings whispering songs praising the wind, the light, the heat, the night of rest, the slow surge of passion waking the fog-cloaked dawn.

"Eat me soon," she tells her love. "Eat me soon."

☆ ☆ ☆

Desire found the Woman in Love living in suburbia, teaching college, married still.

"Shall I go away?" Desire asked, holding herself quietly.

"No," the Woman in Love whispered. "I never did forget."

Swimming at midday in cool water, against the flow, between boulders, Desire smiles at the Woman in Love, tickles her with her toes, races her from shore to shore. Desire pulls her bodice down and squeezes the nipples of the Woman in Love, squeezes and molds her breasts, kisses her with a probing demand, a wanting that will not be stilled. Desire pulls the Woman in Love into the sand and reaches inside her suit, inside her body, pushing her want forward. The Woman in Love pushes back to meet her, to match her, to open to this mating so sun-wrapped, thrust upon her, so longed-for and feared and revered. Coming, she loses contact with all but the radiating sensations centered in her groin, in her ass. Her breath, withheld, she now expels and rocks and burrows into her lover's shoulder, into her lover's breast.

She dreams she is walking through a tunnel constructed of barrel arches. The woman beside her is tall, angular, softened at the edges. They stride in unison, in slow motion, up and down like carousel horses. Sounds form a rolling sea around them. The liquid gathers between her legs, begins its movement downward.

At that shimmering moment when they reenter sunlight, as the sounds rapidly shatter, compelling sensations race outward along her thighs. She feels herself to be both women, inside both women's bodies. The Woman In Love breathes deeply. Both women sigh.

☆ ☆ ☆

Arriving home late one night, the husband of the Woman in Love confronted her with "What would you do if I asked you not to see her any more?"

"Leave you," she said.

☆ ☆ ☆

The Woman in Love returned from the beach alone, bringing polished bones of wood, blue lupine, pebbles filled with light.

Desire met her halfway with small, hungry kisses, smiles, touches soft as moth wings.

"I've decided to leave my husband," the Woman In Love said, whispered, sighed.

"Not because of me, I hope," Desire replied.

"No. No. Because of me."

☆ ☆ ☆

Through winter and the following spring they love:

When you touch me
When I respond
Joy unfolds

You have become my text, my love; your body, your words. I have bound your letters into a volume I carry with me, read at night before I sleep, at dawn before I move into the day.

Your love is a fine spray misting my movements, mellowing my colors, lightening what might have been despair. Where your hands have been, I am yours, and your hands have been everywhere. Your words enter my soil like rain. Your memory, Oh love, your memory takes me suddenly, wrenches me from this world into a fairy tale where I am loved the way I always wanted to be.

☆ ☆ ☆

The Woman in Love dreams and rubs her body against the other's, soft and accessible. She dreams of prairies, wheat fields waving along her torso, streaming in the wind. She wakens to find her hand between the other's legs. Caressing, she imagines she is the first lover there, that they are sixteen-year-olds upstairs at her parent's home, holding each other, undressed, their imaginations excited. Everything is new, intense, iridescent.

Younger, she stretches in a sailboat, the sun all over her, salt spray and foam and constant rocking so that the very earth continues to move when she walks on shore again. She tries out different pictures of herself as a grown-up, finds she wants most to be touched enough, a lot, to be made love to all day.

Her skinny friend comes down the boards to help her tie the boat up, younger, graceful, unselfconscious. She wonders about sex with women, between women, will they ever do more than caress each other's breasts?

She dreams again of the boat as a giant padded cradle protecting and nurturing them as they gently go down on one another, liquid and pliant, spotted with spray.

The boat dissolves into a mountain shrouded in fog where they walk, watching the trees and pathways appear and disappear around them. They find a pool and sub-

126

merge in the streaming warmth, kissing, Oh full lips and hungry loins. Their fingers seek out each other's nipples and rub and squeeze them into exquisite hunger.

They suckle and press, initiating old rituals, reconnecting to a fertile earth where they stretch, slipping fingers into mouths, between their nether lips. They press against the legs and fingers of the other, oblivious. The universe streams out in wisps of foggy thought and sound. Birds announce their coming, cover them with feathers, croon them into dreams within the dreams.

Desire awakens her with coffee, trails fingers along her body, tells her hunger in the touch of her palm. The Woman in Love responds with ardor, pelvis rising without conscious thought. The lover darts her tongue inside, taps excitement's pulse, teasingly withdraws, sustains, intensifies, releases.

☆ ☆ ☆

Seeking herself, the Woman in Love moves on, awakens as day slowly takes the city, flesh pink, pearlescent, aqua, peach. There appears to be neither cloud nor haze crowding her vision. Alone, nude, she moves against the satin comforter fingering her clitoral peak, her breast, her lips. Moistening her vulva, she works her mons with both hands, commandingly, luxuriously. She arches up to meet her fingers; fantasies being kept by a woman in turn-of-the-century Vienna who enters her room to find the Woman in Love pleasuring herself. The keeper, enrapt, pulls the curtain wider at the window, kneels to watch, touch her legs lightly, make contact without intruding.

The Woman in Love comes as her fantasy self responds to hands caressing her, entering her everywhere.

☆ ☆ ☆

Nightmares came, dreams in which her fears rose up, enlarged, distorted, embodied in animals, bugs, reptiles, carnivorous plants, menacing, elongated humanoids. She would pull herself awake, sit up throughout the night saying, "This is what I think. This is who I am. In the dawn the fears will shrink, dissolve. I will endure. I will survive."

Every morning felt like a new beginning.

The nightmares changed form. She would find her dream self running endlessly, never fast enough. Seemingly outside her body, she would watch the dream self flee from terrors her rational mind could never seem to see.

She learned to stop running, to stand and turn to face her torments, to feel herself grown, able to face the trials of a daily world.

Sometimes she would find herself lost in nightmares of confusion, the substance and context of the material world changing, shifting, offering her no safety. People would alter form and character, laugh at her, tease her.

She learned to look them in the eyes, to believe firmly in herself.

☆ ☆ ☆

Fragmentary images of magic cities drift across her mind: Montreal, San Francisco, Philadelphia, Paris, Vancouver, Cincinnati, stone buildings, arches, public sculpture. Streets speckled with sunlight. Food artfully piled in store windows.

Riding the train at twilight, her body appears ephemeral in the glass, cruising backward across the winter landscape. Suddenly, entering a tunnel, she becomes volumetric, subtly yet solidly colored. She flirts with herself, imagines sexual encounters, orgies where beloved hands excite her every sensitivity.

She squeezes her pelvic muscles, considers covering her activity with a coat, seeks out the toilet instead and comes standing, leaning against the wall, her face turned toward the mirror. A long sigh precedes her return to her seat where she sleeps soundly, dreaming of cities.

☆ ☆ ☆

She camped out by oceans, rivers, on wooded mountain sides, ravine edges, alpine meadows.

Meals became picnics: hard boiled eggs, cold fried chicken, peanut butter and strawberry jam on whole wheat bread, päté, brie, stone-ground crackers, sharp cheddars, apples, dark rye, provolone and corned beef with marinated artichokes, dried figs, sourdough, feta, celery, thin sliced spam grilled on a stick over an open fire.

She did odd jobs for money, staying sometimes shorter, sometimes longer times. Always she moved on.

She stretched herself out along the mountains, savoring the Cascade range, the Olympics, the Siskiyous, glorying in the snow-capped giants, the dark bush of the douglas fir, pacific yew, jeffrey and ponderosa pines.

She learned to be at home in her body, to be her own best friend, her favorite lover. Her dreams became clear and luminous, pearlescent, shimmering.

She began to paint again.

☆ ☆ ☆

Sweet anticipation, rising warmly into her awareness, the Woman in Love moved on, wiping her past out behind her for shorter and longer periods of time. Opening herself to the world, the Woman in Love reached out with her attention, her intelligence, her curiosity. Time became immodest, a luxury she squandered exuberantly.

Anticipation awakened her, awakened in her, became the subtle tempo underneath her days.

The memory of Desire, going other places, living other lives, the memory of Desire whispered softly to her, a breeze among the cottonwoods, the cypress, jade and acacia trees. The memory of Desire winked at her from small, starry wildflowers, comforted her when loneliness seemed real.

Sometimes her mind would dream back into the magic words of her childhood: Kissimmee, Lake Okeechobee, the Withlacoochee River, Okefenokee Swamp, Suwannee River, Crystal River, Silver Springs, Apala-

129

chicola, Pensacola, Miami, the Everglades, swamp grass, cattails, sea oats, sand between her toes.

She'd awaken to the magic of the present: Klamath Falls, the Rogue River Valley, Savage Rapids Dam, Lake of the Woods, Trinity Forest, Shasta, Sacramento Delta, Monterey, Mount Madonna, daffodils in winter, mimosas in July.

Memory wove into anticipation, washed across her vision each time she entered a new doorway, crossed a threshold, removed a piece of clothing, dipped her brush in paint. Pleasure: anticipated and remembered, cultivated and savored.

☆ ☆ ☆

In a glory of late morning sunshine, the Woman In Love sits alone in a Victorian-style bar, waiting for a table in the adjoining restaurant. Yellow mums bloom at her elbow, the glass sparkles, glasses shine upside down in rows. She orders almond wine because it's strange to her, sniffs the scent, turns the glass, amber liquid slowly moving; wooden table, parquet floors glow. A woman with a nose like Desire's slinks by in wet-look pants. The walls are green felt, fern-banked. Well-dressed women of her own age pass with their grown daughters, stately, American.

She imagines everyone undressed, fantasizes body hair, freckles, moles. She remembers a lover's evening touch, warmed with oil, sleek and even, rewarding her anticipatory thrill.

The Maître d' leads her to a seat beside a window. She orders, then reads a magazine: facts, raw material for some other dream.

Later, leaving, she notices the scent of a woman she passes, sweet like the flowers of her past. Then night-blooming jasmine vined outside her window, gardenia waited shyly near her door. Voluptuous magnolia with its lemony air stretched its arms above her, concealed her behind glossy leaves. Honeysuckle and confederate jasmine caressed her summer evenings.

She smells again the twice-blooming orange, heady, pervasive. It touched her earliest, deepest memories. Those blossoms, clustering in celebration along the rows in citrus groves invaded her tissues with a joy recreated in even the slightest suggestion of their honeyed odor.

Flowers had bloomed inside her as her first lover, very butch, very gentle, held her hand, quieted her fears, taught her pleasure in the heavy, slow-moving air. Her first lover who held her, night after night, barely touching, breathing in rhythm.

She remembers how they didn't even kiss at first, communicating with small sighs and moans. When one night the lover shifted her weight and carefully covered her, the Woman in Love had sighed with satisfaction, felt completed, safe, home. She'd moved against the other. Both moved as ocean waves, as leaves quiver in the evening breeze. They moved against each other, breathed and dreamed. Lying back, she'd flowered within the other's hands, exploded like the night-blooming cereus, unfolding rapidly into the dark, perfuming the air with the odor of her love. Years later she wrote: "Did you want my heart to stop when you came all dressed in white?"

"Yes," the other answered. "Yes."

☆ ☆ ☆

Sleeping, the Woman in Love dreams that morning massages her with peach-colored fingers, nails painted aqua; a fairy silk, midnight garment trailing stars behind her as morning rubs knotted muscles, frees tightened ligaments, realigns her spine.

Morning claims her as her own work of art, painting her in broad strokes, slick with pigment. Outlining her figure, simplifying the background, the structure, the womanly form. She highlights the face, the hands, heart and groin then hands the brush to the Woman in Love, flutters lightly across her face saying, "Today, reach into the world today."

The Woman in Love takes her portfolio and fastens pictures to the walls and fences of the city: pictures of women loving, giant flowers, cunts like sea shells, like fish swimming. She hums as she moves, dreaming still, slow dancing through the early streets.

☆ ☆ ☆

The Woman in Love awoke to autumn, the ginkgo's leaves a yellow skirt around her trunk, floppy bright maple, aspen gold, oak: red and yellow, green and brown.

The Woman in Love awoke and knew her wanderings were over, her roots sunk deep in her own psychic soil. No matter where she went from here, she would always be home.

Autumn spread itself around her, marigold orange and rust, the last of the geraniums, early violets, milkweed seeds in the wind.

Mushrooms dotted the ground, some shouting for attention, others blending, hiding, teasing her.

Cones matured and fell from white and shasta firs, western hemlock, brewer spruce, sugar and lodgepole pine. Golden chinquapin dropped burry nuts among the leaves and scattered berries, madrone fleshed out in anticipation.

The Woman in Love awoke to autumn, specific, extravagant, unique, singing a song of joy.

☆ ☆ ☆

"You know, I always forget the pungent smell of punk wood trees in bloom, the outrageousness of bird of paradise, salt water in my mouth, salt dusting my skin.

"Memory seems to come so easily to me that I mourn the smells, the images that I know I've lost. I feel pierced when I encounter them again.

"Memory," she said, "is an archive, a resource, a library of the senses. Each pattern, taste, smell opening onto others.

"Memories," she said, "make noticing in the first place all the more worthwhile. Yet, the older I've gotten, the more I discard by forgetting. And this forgetting seems to be freeing me. It's as if I can finally afford to forget. The monsters, fears, terrors of my past are buried in my past, decomposing, composting, metamorphosed into fertilizer in that slow organic way that living sometimes brings.

"Lighter," she said, "I feel so much lighter now and filled with energy."

She dreams repeatedly of the white flowers of her childhood — fading — the flowered dresses, halter tops, pedal pushers becoming pale, bleached by time, the flowers, pale ghosts of flowers, dissolve into a muted sky, wispy, violet shadows pressed flat within the pages of her mind.

She honors them one final time, then folds the layers of her memory and opens her eyes to a new day.

☆ ☆ ☆

The Woman in Love met Desire again in London, sitting in a pub, slim, graying, full of stories. They returned to her flat, undressed almost shyly, excited still. Beneath the sheets they continued talking, touched slowly, hesitantly; joked about their mouths being dry.

When the Woman in Love buried her face in the other's shoulder, the hands of Desire were freed to move over her, opening her again.

"So long," she said. "It's been so long since we've been together, since it's been like this for me."

That first coming together, again and again, over distances beyond her imagination, compelled awe. The adequacy of a cheek, a touch, became fire and hunger, sweat and love.

The Woman in Love moaned.

The Woman in Love sighed.

Desire raged and washed over her. This time they both came.

In the morning the Woman in Love woke first, turned to kiss her lover, found her quiet and still. The Woman In Love feared morning would take what the night had given, touched her lover's shoulder lightly and willed herself returned to sleep. She dreamed of beaches, of walking alone on windswept ocean beaches, looking for someone.

☆ ☆ ☆

She dreams the wind is blowing off the water, reaching through her clothes, drawing the hair from her face. Morning explodes, coral and flushed, exposing multiple horizons. Gulls flash and circle, calling to her, teasingly, to join them. She lifts from the sand, elongating her body, stretching her muscles, reaching out.

Soaring higher, she wants to thank the birds, the morning, but finds she cannot speak. The rosy gilt-edged hands of day encompass her, wrap around her, turn her, mold the furry ravine between her legs, Behind the dreamer's dream eyes, novas explode, the day breaks in two, freeing shooting stars across a velvet sky. The dreamer gasps and twines her fingers in the heliotrope hair of day. An early breeze kisses her cheeks, flutters a curtain lightly across her face. Stretching, she soars again, glides and turns, coupling with the wind.

Nearing Desire, excitement rises, circles within her torso, whistles in her head. Dreaming, she crashes into the other's shore, rolls and turns across her beaches, kites and dips along the other's bony spine.

Desire erupts into a twilight sky to meet her, flowing down her own sides, winking, fiery. Warm breath, lava-flecked, encases her extended body, claiming her.

The Woman in Love awakened to find herself enfolded. Oh, those body smells! warm touch, firm hands. "Oh, god," said the Woman in Love. "Thank you, god," she said and looked into the other's eyes, liquid, calm and close.

They ate oranges in Valencia and bathed in the sea.

In Barcelona they lived in a small, cool, white room; wandered among the flower vendors until, aroused beyond propriety, they returned to their room and drank each other's bodies, breathed each other's smells.

134

Their honeymoon lasted as long as they needed. When their work drew them back to America, they returned, alone, together.

OTHER BOOKS FROM BANNED BOOKS

Cass and the Stone Butch,
  Antoinette Azolakov $8.95
Death Strip,
  Benita Kirkland $8.95
A Cry in the Desert,
  Jed A. Bryan $9.95

BANNED BOOKS
Number 231, P.O. Box 33280, Austin, Texas 78764